I0733750

REACHING INTO SILENCE

By Linda Sammaritan

ISBN-13: 978-1-959788-08-9

This book is dedicated to my father,
Philip G. Geib, the man whose rock-solid faith
and calm outlook on life
taught me to trust God for
everything.

The Lord has given me the passion to write. With
gratitude and praise, I offer this gift to Him.

Acknowledgments

Although *Reaching Into Silence* must be considered a work of fiction, many of the episodes are true, and I could never have remembered so many bits and pieces of our childhood without the help of my brothers and sister—Doug, Steve, and Tricia, the real Paul, Wade, and Krista.

My mother has been my greatest cheerleader, and she and Tricia have also been my keenest critics:

"I don't remember it happening that way."

"It's fiction, Mom."

"Why can't my name be Marie?"

"Because 'Marie' is too easy for a deaf kid to say."

"You missed a comma."

(I missed several. I hope we corrected all of them.)

I'm grateful for my husband who has watched my writing grow from a vague dream of storytelling to baby steps in learning to write to seeing my words in print. He never complains when I ignore pots and pans soaking in the sink and tap on my computer keys instead and has let me know in a zillion ways how proud he is of me.

Special thanks to friends who encouraged me to write, especially Danette who kept saying, "This is a story that needs to be told." So I did.

The World Without Sound series has endured several revisions, and I'm forever grateful to all who combed through every line: Linda who edited the original version, and Molly and Jessica who loved the characters and helped me make them better.

Thank you, Heartland writers. John, Joyce, Cheryl,

Amber, Savannah, Michele, Mary Kay, Janie, Anne, Beth, and several who joined us off and on. Your encouragement and prayers and knowledge of publishing have enabled me to soldier on as I step onto a public platform!

Thank you to my Indy Writers Meet-Up Group—Steve, Rich, James, Marianne, Tom, Doug, Greg, Krish, and Sasha—you've seen this from the beginning. And to Michael, Jerry, Richard, Sandee, John, and Jeff, you helped me to polish it as we reached the end.

I will never be able to offer enough thanks to my wonderful Scriblerians who invited me into their critique group and have taught me so much— Beth, Cynthia, Tim, Karen, Gretchen, Lisa, Loraine, Kathrese, and Vanessa. You were my first writing "family," and you will always hold a special place in my heart.

To my student beta readers—Kyle, Caleb, Ashlyn, DiAra, Rachel, MacKenzie, Jonathan, Olivia, and Joshua— you allowed me to see how kids would view this book. Read it again. It's much better because of your comments!

Lady Lits, you are quickly becoming dear friends and mentors! Nancy, Sarah, Susan, Mari, Jill, Janet, and Jessica, I have learned so much from you in the past year. I appreciate your encouraging words and individual skill sets. You cheer me on to the finish line.

Finally, thank you, Cynthia Hickey and Winged Publications, for believing in the value of this story.

A Note to the Deaf Community

The World Without Sound series begins in 1965 and ends in 1970. At that time, the medical and educational establishments were convinced sign language did more harm than good, believing deaf children would never learn to communicate with the hearing world.

These were years where the schools demanded "speech only" education. Hearing parents, deaf children, and many teachers ended up feeling even more defeated in an already-frustrating situation. It wasn't until later in the Seventies that ASL was considered an acceptable alternative, and my sister's school taught both sign language and speech. I believe the combination was labeled "total communication," although today, that term includes cued speech, SEE, and other sign languages.

While I have noticed some contention on both trains of thought to this day, I believe ASL is more accepted as a viable means of communication, and our deaf children grow up with far less stress.

A Note to the 21st Century Reader

Language evolves with each generation. What was an acceptable word or phrase in another century or even five years ago, may be condemned as derogatory or hateful today.

To be true to the era of the 1960s, you may find some of my terminology offensive, particularly the label of "mentally retarded." However, the term was acceptable to both medical and educational professionals. In fact, my first state teaching license contained these words as my specialty: "Mildly Mentally Retarded."

In the World Without Sound series, I considered changing the term to "cognitively challenged" or "developmentally disabled," but modern phrases throw the reader into present times instead of what the world was really like fifty years ago and more.

Within the narrative, I have tried to make sure the reader understands which words were medically appropriate and which were intended as insults. And believe me, main character Debbie more than bristles at the cruelty she occasionally meets in others!

REACHING INTO SILENCE

Chapter 1:
German Measles (June 1965)

All is dark, silent.
I yawn, I stretch, I float in
My warm, salty lake.

If I'd known we were celebrating the first day of summer vacation with cheese Danish, I might've put down my book and run for breakfast an hour ago.

Mom handed me the plate bordered with little blue seashells but didn't leave the room. Instead, she sat on the sofa across from me, which made the round bump of her belly more noticeable. After two little brothers, maybe I'd get a sister this time. I could hardly wait. A sister would make a great birthday present.

Mom patted the place beside her, indicating I should join her. A serious discussion must be in the works. Back when I was ten, she'd invited me to sit next to her for a "little talk" about girls becoming young ladies. I hoped she wasn't about to have another "little talk" that would leave me wishing to disappear from embarrassment. To avoid eye contact, I perched on the edge of the cushion and focused on each mouthful of sweet, cream cheese filling from my Danish.

Mom heaved one of those sighs I'd gotten used to since last winter. "Debbie, I know you're happy about the new baby, but I need to tell you something."

What would make me *un*happy about the baby? I switched my attention from the Danish to her face, searching for a clue. She attempted a smile but gave up, and I glanced away to avoid the worry in her eyes.

What if the *something* she needed to tell me about was something wrong with *her?* She'd been acting weird lately, never smiling, staring off into space, and not noticing stuff going on right in front of her. In fact, just the other day, she let my seven-year-old brother, Wade, eat *ten* sandwich cookies. Ten. We hadn't even had breakfast. My normal mother, Mrs. Eggs and Toast, would have never let that happen.

I licked the last smidgen of Danish off my fingers and wiped them on my pajamas before I dared to finally look straight at Mom. Her bright red lipstick contrasted with her dark hair and eyes making her movie-star beautiful. People even compared her to Jackie Kennedy, one of the most glamorous women alive. My mom was more than just beautiful—she was a stunner, inside and out, as Daddy always said.

What if Mom was going to lose the baby the way the First Lady had? I tried to swallow the sudden lump that had formed in my throat. Everybody had cried when the President got shot, but I cried for poor Mrs. Kennedy. First, she lost the new baby, and then she lost her husband. And I sure didn't want to be in the same boat as poor little Caroline Kennedy who lost her father *and* her baby sister.

Mom sighed again and stroked the satiny, raised paisley pattern on the couch while I twined my fingers together and squeezed hard like they'd crush any bad news to death.

"There might be something wrong with the baby." She stared at her fingertip as it followed the lines of green and blue swirls. "In fact, the doctor says it probably won't be *normal*." Her voice cracked as she spoke that last word. As if *normal* was something delicate, like fine crystal and easily shattered.

Her words didn't make sense. No one could even *see* the baby yet. I peered at Mom's stomach trying to picture a teeny-tiny infant curled up in there. Sound asleep. *Safe*.

Mom was fine. She just needed to find a different doctor instead of the quack she'd been going to.

"How can anybody know if there's something wrong with a baby before it's born?" I asked, folding my arms across my chest.

A single tear rolled to her chin, and she let it drop, as if she didn't have the energy to brush it off her face.

I shifted my gaze to the window. I hadn't meant to make her cry, but if Doctor Quack had been in the room, I would've lit into him so hard his liar, liar pants on fire would've flamed to the ceiling.

In a softer voice, I asked, "Why does he say the baby won't be normal?"

"Do you remember when your brothers had German measles back in January? And then I got it, too?"

"Yes." I remembered clearly because everyone had gotten a rash and swollen glands except for me and Daddy.

"That's why we know something's wrong… because I had German measles when the baby was first beginning to grow inside of me." She dabbed at her eyes with a tissue and wadded it into a tight ball.

"But you were hardly sick at all," I protested. "The boys weren't that sick either."

"It may not seem like much when you catch it, but rubella—German measles—damages babies who aren't born yet." She brushed away a few strands of blond hair tickling my cheek. "I want you to be ready." Mom squared her shoulders like a soldier preparing to march into battle. "This baby could be blind or deaf. Other things could be wrong, too. We won't know until after it's born."

A baby who will never see? Never hear? Something *worse*?

Her words buzzed around me like a swarm of bees, alighting on my brain and immediately lifting off in swirling, paisley patterns of their own. If I stayed *really* still and didn't act scared, maybe none of those words would sting me.

Problems like this happened to heroes in stories, not to regular people like us. Besides, God wouldn't let awful things happen to our family. *Would* He?

And if He did, maybe there would be a miracle. In Sunday school, we always heard stories about Jesus healing blind people and deaf people. If God did miracles back then, He could do the same things now.

Mom grasped my chin, so I had to look into her eyes. "Do you understand what I'm trying to tell you?"

No. Not really. I nodded anyway.

"Daddy and I want you to be ready for whatever could happen. I know you've been so excited that you're old enough to help with this baby. We may need a lot more help than any of us bargained for." She leaned over and hugged me. "Do you have any questions?"

I shook my head no. I had too many questions to count. Where would I begin?

Chapter 2:
In the Closet of My Mind

Motion from outside
Jolts me awake. I frown, tense,
Then settle in sleep.

The windows were all the way open, but not a wisp of a breeze reached me, and kicking off the sheet only made it worse. I *hated* lying in bed with no covers, because nothing soaked up the sweat dripping all over my arms and legs.

My sandpaper tongue tempted me with the vision of a pitcher filled with ice cold water. I slipped downstairs and tiptoed into the kitchen, the linoleum floor cool beneath my feet. Moonlight reflected on the faucet as I filled a glass. I took a seat on one of the maple chairs at the table. The heat from my legs warmed the wood too quickly, but the glass was cold, and I held it against my cheek before taking another sip.

After the "talk" with Mom last month, I had shoved the idea of a *not-normal* baby to some dark corner of my brain—kind of like stuffing old toys into the back of my closet--but sitting here alone in the middle of the night, I pulled out the *not-normal* baby thoughts from the closet of my mind.

What would things be like in a few years? I had imagined a little sister with light brown pigtails and a freckled face. Maybe as many freckles as Wade. She'd be skinnier than me, of course, and more of a tomboy. I didn't have an athletic bone in my body. Surely, she'd be able to throw a baseball farther than I could, and she'd run a fifty-yard dash in less than ten seconds.

Since I already had two brothers, I never pictured myself taking care of a baby boy. Paul and Wade were rowdy enough.

I desperately needed a sister.

A sister would be a reading buddy. My brothers would rather stack books into towers and knock them down. Sisters liked to gab about everything and nothing. Paul and Wade only talked about sports—from their latest exploits on the field to the value of a Mickey Mantle card.

My sister and I would be best friends, even better friends than Francie and me.

But—

We were supposed to play piano duets together. How could a deaf girl play the piano? She'd never know if she hit a wrong note.

We were supposed to read *Dana Girls* mysteries together. A blind girl couldn't go to the library and pick out a book. Wouldn't she need to find a special library with braille books?

One of the *something worse* things Mom and Daddy had talked about was mental retardation. Why did I think of that as *something worse*? Was it worse than walking around in the dark all day and all night without even a lit match to offer some light? Worse than isolation in a bubble of silence that never allowed a whisper of melody to enter?

Did it seem worse because those two words sounded so awful together? Separately, they were fine. *Mental.* Something done with the mind. *Retardation.* When something slows down. Like *ritardando* written on sheet music, and I slow down the tempo as I play the piano. But put both words side by side, and what do you get? *The mind that is slowed down.*

Actually, when I analyzed it like that, it didn't sound so bad. Maybe people's reactions were the problem. They know that leading a blind person in the wrong direction is downright mean. The same with doing something sneaky behind a deaf person. But they tend to laugh at a slow person. When the mind is slow, it takes longer to understand a joke. It takes longer to learn anything. Like reading books.

What if my sister would never be able to read at all? That might be the *worst* thing. I would be so mad at God if He let that happen to us.

As I held the cold glass of water to my face, a thousand pictures of pain tumbled out of the closet of my mind. Pictures of my sister stumbling over chairs set in her path or tripping over a tree root on a forest path, walking into walls, falling off a curb into traffic. Pictures of her riding a bike and never hearing the truck that knocks her off the road or getting in trouble for ignoring the teacher's directions. Pictures of a little girl surrounded by bullies who pinch her arms, and she has no idea why they are acting like that when all she wanted was to be friends.

That last thought brought on a cascade of tears. It had really happened to some poor little girl on the base playground a couple of years ago. Would my little sister have to endure something so horrible?

And no matter which *not-normal* we had to deal with, it would affect the rest of the family. I would be known as the girl with the deaf sister or the girl with the blind sister or the girl with the mentally retarded sister. None of those would bother me, exactly, except kids get mean.

They'll jab at me with stupid questions like, "Does your sister drool all over herself?"

It was okay for doctors to say a *patient* was mentally retarded. They were describing a medical condition. But when bullies called you a *retard,* they wanted to see you cry. What was *wrong* with people? If someone called my sister one of those names, *I* would cry, maybe even punch them in the face.

My empty glass proved that water went right through my system. I needed the bathroom, so I stuffed those awful thoughts back in the closet of my mind and tiptoed down the hall, trying to keep the floorboards from creaking as I passed my parent's bedroom. No need to explain why I was awake.

"I can feel him moving." Daddy chuckled. "Pretty active kid for once."

Him? Daddy wanted another boy? I halted like I was in a game of Freeze Tag.

Mom giggled. "Yeah, when I feel those kicks, I'm so glad he's alive. But a moment later, I'm worrying about what handicaps the poor child will have to deal with." Her voice ended in a little sob.

"It's going to be okay, sweetheart." Daddy talked to her like she was a baby herself.

"Maybe we should have gone to Sweden."

"No. Sweden wasn't the answer. We would've never forgiven ourselves."

Why would they go to Sweden? Had they wanted to give away the baby?

"We'll get through this. You'll see." Daddy's voice was firm.

"But our lives are never going to be the same."

Another chuckle. "Our lives were never the same after Debbie was born. Then Paul changed things. And then Wade."

"This is different." Mom blew her nose, a liquid-y huff into a tissue. "Before, we expected good things, our three little blessings. Now we're expecting bad things."

Sheets rustled and the mattress springs squeaked as someone's weight shifted on the bed before Daddy responded. "Maybe you should say we're expecting *difficult* things. Nothing about this baby is *bad*."

"Difficult things *are* bad."

"No, they're not," he argued. "They're just, well, difficult. It's like when I'm flying toward a storm system. We have all the necessary information, and we make a plan to avoid the worst of the turbulence."

"A handicapped child is not the same as a run-of-the-mill thunderstorm."

He snorted. "Tell me that the next time you fly right through one of those monsters." Silence. "Anyway, we know this storm is coming, and after the baby's born, we'll make a plan, no matter how difficult the challenges become. We're not in this alone, you know."

I didn't hear the rest as I hurried to the bathroom. I couldn't hold it any longer.

Back in bed, a cricket lullaby made me drowsy. All the worries that skittered through my mind like an open bag of marbles rolling across the kitchen floor slowed to a standstill as Daddy's words calmed the fear. "A change. A storm. A plan. We're not alone."

Life had changed for my parents every time they added a kid. Would it be such a big deal for us to change some things? *Was* it so terrible to live with a handicapped person? When I was in fourth grade, my teacher was blind. Everyone had hoped to get into her class. She had a great seeing-eye dog, and she taught us the braille alphabet. If I could learn the alphabet, I could learn to read braille and teach my little sister. Maybe we would get her a seeing-eye dog.

Mr. and Mrs. Davidson from across the street were deaf. Their two kids could hear, and just like regular families they talked to each other, except they did it with their hands.

Now when I thought about my daydreams, my little sister kept the pigtails and the scraped knees of a tomboy, and we would still be best friends. If she ended up deaf, we'd talk with our hands. If she was blind, we'd learn to read with our hands. If her mind was slow, I would teach her to read… no matter how long it took. This baby could be born with six heads, green skin, and covered in warts, and we'd love her anyway. Even if *she* turned out to be a *he*.

I still had a couple of months before I had to deal with any of the doctor's predictions. A more immediate problem was rushing toward me. Something I'd tried not to think about all summer. Saying goodbye to my best friend Francie.

Chapter 3:
Empty Spaces

Rhythm and bouncing.
Skinny fingers wave at me.
Catch one in my mouth.

We'd been in constant motion all day. Mom strode from room to room, directing the movers while Dad checked each box on the master list as it went out the front door. By dinner time, the house was empty, and I was allowed to stay overnight with Francie for one last time--my reward for helping to clean all day.

Mrs. Capelli, Francie's mom, made lasagna, my favorite, but the lump in my throat didn't let me swallow more than a few little bites. Francie didn't eat much either. After dinner, we joined the rest of the neighborhood kids in a game of Tag. My brothers' absence just made it more obvious that I would never play that game again with Francie. She must have felt the same way, because when our eyes met, we nodded to each other and ran down the street, away from the game. In the twilight, we walked and cried, and cried and walked. We went back to her house and turned on the television. That way we wouldn't look at each other. It didn't matter. A side glance showed me her face was wet with tears, and I kept wiping mine with the back of my hand.

Mrs. Capelli finally ordered us to bed. She was my mother's best friend, and she treated me like her own kid. So, we put on our pajamas and crawled under the covers. I gazed at every object, memorizing this room that I might never stay in again. The pink walls, the rosebud bedspreads, the white furniture, and the overstuffed chair holding most of Francie's teddy bears. She still slept with two.

Once again, salty tears reached trembling lips. Not even thoughts of my soon-to-be-born sister made me feel better. I should have gone to the hotel with my family. If I had stayed with them, we'd be in one big huddle on the bed watching TV. I'd be snuggled under Daddy's arm, Wade would be snuggled under Mom's arm, and Paul would sit between the two of them, pretending he was too old to snuggle.

Mrs. Capelli pulled the sheet up to my chin and kissed my forehead. Her perfume smelled spicier than Mom's. "You promise to write to us, right?" she asked in a whisper.

I nodded and sniffled back more tears.

Instead of telling me to stop crying like *my* mom would, she handed me a tissue. "Remember. We *will* see each other again." She held up her index finger. "*You* will come up here for a winter vacation and enjoy all of our snow." She pointed her finger at the other bed, "And *Francie* and the rest of us will visit you next summer and swim in the ocean.”

Perfect words I needed to hear. Thinking about the ocean calmed me down. Even though the waves terrified me with their amazing power, I still loved to stand on the shore and watch them break, rush over my feet, and return to the sea. The ocean was the one thing that made me happy about this move.

Mrs. Capelli stepped to Francie’s bed, handed her a tissue, too, and tucked her in with another kiss. She turned out the light, and with a whispered good night, shut the door. Sometimes, I wished Francie and I could trade mothers.

I talked into the darkness. “You and me at the beach. I kind of like that idea. And by summer, you’ll get to meet the new baby.”

“That’s not for a whole year.” Francie’s voice sounded scratchy. “What do we do between now and then?”

There really wasn’t a good answer to that question. No matter how many letters we wrote or how many long-distance phone calls our parents would be willing to pay for, nothing was ever going to be the same. I was moving away. Francie was staying behind. We had no say in the matter.

The lump in my throat swelled until I could barely get words out. “For the first time in my life, I wish my dad wasn’t in the Air Force.”

“Yeah. Air Force kids always move away.”

I rubbed the silky sheet between my thumb and pointer finger, thinking of the many moves we’d already made as a military family. “Before we came here, we used to move twice a year, and I liked it, but you’ve been my best friend for two whole years now.

It's a lot harder to leave this time."

"I don't think I want any more Air Force friends. Ever." Francie blew her nose into the tissue.

Those words brought new tears to my eyes. "But what if we *hadn't* ever been friends? We wouldn't have crawled through the hole in the backyard fence. We wouldn't have had sleepovers. We wouldn't have played Barbies. Or Mother May I. Or Red Light, Green Light. We wouldn't have gone to the drive-in movies."

The movie nights were the best, camped out in the back of a station wagon with our brothers, lying on blankets smelling of grass, dirt, and sweat. We always munched on popcorn—extra butter—and giggled over private jokes. Often, we sneaked peeks at the second feature long after we were supposed to be asleep.

Those memories didn't comfort Francie, though. "If we'd never been friends, I wouldn't know what I missed. Maybe I would've had another best friend who was almost as much fun as you."

I wanted to be mad at her, but I kind of knew how she felt. I hated being left behind. When I lived in Niagara Falls, I wanted to move when my friend did. When I looked at her empty house across the street and her empty desk in the classroom, it left an empty space in my heart.

Francie's breathing evened out. She must have cried herself to sleep. The drone of the television downstairs and the familiar hint of garlic in the air reminded me this had been my home away from home. I propped myself up on one elbow and peeked out the window next to the bed. There stood my old house, empty, dark, and barely visible in the moonless night— no longer my home.

That fact somehow made it easier to turn away, ready to start my new adventure. I'd have a new school, a new sister, and a new home near the ocean. Francie would have the same old house, the same old brother, and the same old school. Every time she looked across her backyard, she'd see her best friend's house, only her best friend wouldn't be in it.

I relaxed against the pillow. The sheer curtains whispered in the breeze that caressed my face. Before I dropped off, I figured out what I could leave behind to help fill the empty space in Francie's heart. Hopefully, every time she looked at it, she would remember our friendship and what could have been.

The next morning, I woke up way too early, for a lot of reasons: not in my own house, not in my own bed, and not sure if I ever really went to sleep at all. Birds called to one another in the dawn's light. When Francie finally stumbled her way to the downstairs bathroom, I hopped out of bed, opened my overnight case, and plucked out my Tressy doll.

Francie had been the last one to style Tressy's hair, pressing the button on the doll's back, which allowed her to pull the hair as long as it would go. Then she had wound small locks of hair to create all kinds of curls and pinned them to Tressy's head. All the doll needed was an evening gown, and she'd be ready for the prom.

Mom had hinted I might be getting too old for dolls, but I insisted on taking this one in the car. Along with books, I could pass some of the time on the long drive perfecting Tressy's braid.

Most of the girls in our class *had* stopped playing with dolls. Or at least, that's what they said. But Francie and I still enjoyed dressing up our Barbies and even playing house with old baby dolls, though we would never advertise the fact at school.

Tressy wouldn't be traveling to the ocean with me, after all. Her elaborate coiffure proved Francie was much better at styling Tressy's hair anyway. All I could ever manage was a sloppy braid or combing it out long and smooth.

I needed to hurry. The clinks and clanks from the kitchen signaled I'd soon be called to breakfast.

Francie's closet was stuffed with old toys, books, art supplies, and clothes, both on hangers and on the floor. She even had a Susie Homemaker Oven along the side wall. What a contrast from what I left behind yesterday, a closet holding nothing but the sharp odor of mothballs.

I grabbed a coloring book and box of crayons and wrote on an unused page in red. "Debbie says I can stay." Then I ripped the page from the book and folded it lots of times until it fit inside the front of Tressy's dress.

A single sausage curl artfully framed Tressy's cheek. For the last time, I wrapped the curl around my pinkie, and then allowed the hair to slide off. I set the doll in a corner of the closet and shut the door just before Francie walked back into the room.

"Mom is making waffles."

Our favorite breakfast. We got dressed, and she carried my overnight case downstairs for me. We didn't talk. We didn't cry. I guess all things come to an end, even tears.

Chapter 4:
Baby Names

Rhythm and bouncing
Have stopped. The walls are too close.
My house is too small.

On our ten-hour drive across New York State to Long Island, we stopped at a rest area. We'd been pretty comfortable in the car all morning, but the afternoon was heating up. Daddy handed each of us a dime, and we ran to the stone building that housed bathrooms and vending machines to pick a soda. Each of us chose a different plastic button to push, and *voilá,* a new bottle appeared. I helped Wade twist his under the cap opener. When it hissed at the release of pressure, we both smiled in satisfaction. Sweet and icy. Just what we needed.

Paul started to climb back into the station wagon. He'd put up with hours in a hot car and hardly any breaks just to get there and be done with it.

Daddy paused from cleaning bugs off the windshield. "We don't leave here until you're done with the sodas and visit the restrooms."

Mom added, "No sticky messes in the car." She pointed to an empty table under a huge tree. "Time for lunch."

Nobody said much as we sat around the splintered table, tipping the bottles to our mouths, and inhaling late summer greenery combined with truck exhaust. I kept the open top covered with my hand between sips. That helped keep the bees away, something I learned the hard way when I was a little kid.

Wade smacked his lips as he swallowed a bite of peanut butter and jelly. "I want to play *What to Name the Baby.*"

Our favorite family game for the summer.

Paul drained the last of his root beer and wiped his mouth with the back of his hand. "How about Bowser for a boy?"

Wade howled with laughter. "*Ow-oooo!* My brother the dog. How about Bowser Grant? Bowser Grant Hansen."

Daddy stuck his nose in the air and huffed. "I refuse to put my name next to a dog's."

We giggled some more.

"How about Henry Herbert Hansen?" I said. "All H's."

"Make it Huey, like the cartoon duck." Paul stood on the picnic bench. "Huey Herbert Hansen. Then when Mom calls him home for dinner, she'll sound like a farmer calling the pigs." He demonstrated. "Hyoo-oo-oo-*eeeey!*"

The sound bounced to the woods and back. People at nearby tables dotted across the grass turned to look at us. Mostly, they were grinning, but one old man glared our way, marched to his car, and slammed the door when he got in.

Mom smiled. "Your voice carries, kiddo." She gathered up apple cores and wax paper wrappings from the sandwiches. "Okay. A boy can be Huey. But you're not going to catch me calling pigs any time soon."

"Now, a girl's name." Wade slurped more of his cream soda.

"I want something exotic," I said, blinking up toward the cloudless, blue sky over our heads. "Like… Marguerite."

"*Ewww,*" Paul pinched his nose with two fingers. "What do you put with something as icky-sweet as Mar-gue-rite?" He'd turned the name into a poem.

"It's *French*. And I already thought about a middle name. Marguerite Pearl."

"Disgusting." Of course, Wade always sided with Paul.

I stuck out my tongue and glowered at them.

Daddy stepped in before I could say anything nasty. "Okay, for today we have a disgusting French gem for a girl or an overgrown duck for a boy."

With that picture in my head, I had to let go of my mad and laugh.

Back on the road, my bare legs stuck to the vinyl seat, and hot, dusty wind rushed through the car. At least it kept the hair off my neck and dried the sweat. The rumble of tires on pavement reminded me of the miles stretching between Francie and me. I wanted to escape into a book before I started to cry, but Mom started up the baby name game again. For real this time. Maybe that would keep my mind off my troubles.

"I still like Diana Jeanne very much," Mom said. "Let's stick with that."

I argued my case. "It hasn't worked *twice*. First, you wanted Paul or Diana, and we got Paul. Then you chose Wade or Diana, and we got Wade. If you keep Diana for a girl's name, the baby will turn out to be a boy. I say we drop Diana."

"But I haven't heard another name I like." She sighed. "What do you think, Grant?"

Daddy tapped his fingers on the steering wheel, then shrugged. "Let's hear some serious suggestions. I like Doris, but no one else seems to care for it."

"That's right. You almost named *me* Doris." I made a face. "Nobody gets named that anymore. I don't think I would've ever forgiven you if you called me that. Or worse, Dottie." I gave a little kick to the back of his seat.

"Dottie never appealed to me either," Mom agreed.

"Now your mom, she is definitely a Dorothy. Like in the *Wizard of Oz*. She took me over the rainbow, that's for sure." Daddy wiggled his eyebrows at her. "She still does."

Mom smacked his shoulder. "Keep your eyes on the road, Romeo."

I liked it when they got romantic.

Paul rolled his eyes. "Yuck." He bent down to pluck a Matchbox car from the floor littered with a dozen of the things.

Wade rolled his eyes, too, and echoed the yuck but looked puzzled. "How about Leigh Ann?" No distractions kept him from What to Name the Baby.

Paul snickered. "Just because Leigh Ann's your girlfriend doesn't mean we have to name a sister after her."

Wade blushed to the roots of his white-blond hair. "Leigh Ann is *not* my girlfriend."

"Yes, she is." Paul taunted him in a singsong voice. "Wade loves Leigh Aaa-annn, Wade loves Leigh Aaa-annn."

Wade punched him in the ribs. Paul punched back, making sure the little car's bumper stuck out between two fingers of his fist. Wade yelped and rubbed his sweaty arm.

Mom sighed. Again. "Boys, don't get started. Paul, stop teasing him. And Wade, there's no need to get upset about liking a girl."

"I *don't* like Leigh Ann," Wade muttered. "She stinks."

"I don't think Leigh Ann is a name I like well enough anyway," Daddy said. Using the rearview mirror, he watched the boys quietly pinching each other. "Case closed, boys." The firmness in his voice warned them of future consequences if they didn't stop it.

Paul dropped the car onto the seat beside me. My hand closed over it. One last glare exchanged between the boys, and all was calm again.

Mom asked, "How about something simple like Anne or Jane?" She wrinkled her nose. "No, I don't like Jane. But how about Anne?"

Daddy shook his head. "Anne Hansen sounds like a ladies' clothing line at Sears."

"You don't like *anything* I come up with." Mom lifted her chin in exasperation and fanned her neck with a folded road map.

"I like Diana." He was maddeningly smug.

"No." Mom and I answered at the same time. Ah. Mom agreed with me. She wanted a girl but wouldn't say so.

A beautiful name entered my head. I didn't know anyone by that name, but I'd heard of it. Somewhere.

"How about Krista?" I asked the question very quietly, then held my breath hoping for a positive response. I *wanted* this name. It was perfect. And if Paul said one mean thing about it, his car was going out the window. My fist curled around his treasure.

"Krista." Mom rolled the name over her tongue.

Everybody repeated it a couple of times, trying it out.

"I like it," said Wade.

Paul added, "Me, too. That's a good one. Krista Hansen."

My hand slowly descended to the floor, and I allowed the car to roll out of my grip.

"I think I like it too," Mom mused. "Krista sounds very pretty. What middle name would you put with Krista?"

I thought for a moment. "Each time before we had Diana Jeanne. I think Krista Jeanne sounds just as nice."

"Oh, yes." Mom sounded pleased. "Krista Jeanne Hansen. I like it."

Daddy hadn't said anything yet.

"Daddy, is Krista as nice a name as Diana?" I asked.

"I'm thinking." He stared ahead at the highway, one hand on the wheel, the other hanging out the window letting the wind stream through his fingers.

I waited. Either we finally had a name for a baby girl, *my* name for her, or one more possibility bit the dust because of Daddy.

"I like the name, but… it's not really a proper name. It's more of a nickname."

I slumped in my seat, the bubble of hope growing inside my heart was about to burst. I wanted to kick the back of the driver's seat, hard, this time. If Daddy insisted on Diana, I was doomed to brother number three.

He went on. "Why don't we name her Christina Jeanne? A traditional name."

"But Christina sounds too grown up for a little baby," I objected. "And you would spell it with a *Ch*. I want Krista with a *K*."

"She'll grow into her name."

Mom sided with me. "I wouldn't want to call her Christina, either. And I don't like Chris. People wouldn't know if she was a boy or a girl." She leaned toward Daddy. "If you like the name Krista, why can't we just name her Krista?"

"Because Krista's a nickname." Then he smiled. "Let's name her Christina Jeanne Hansen with a C, but we'll always call her Krista. With a *K*. How's that?"

"I love it!" I threw the book into the air in celebration.

Wade snagged it before it landed on his head. He gave me a dirty look and chucked it all the way to the back of the station wagon.

I didn't mind. I bounced in my seat and sang at the top of my lungs. "We've got a Krista. I've got a sis-tuh. We've got a Krista. I've got a sis-tuh."

Mom pecked Daddy on the cheek. She turned to look at me over the seat. "Not so loud, Debbie."

She rarely had to tell *me* to lower my voice.

A sudden thought cut my song short. If Krista ended up not liking her name, it would be all my fault.

Chapter 5:
Nancy

Feet push against walls.
Finally, no more thrum-thrum.
Dim, translucent light.

Under a bright blue sky and a few cotton ball clouds, our station wagon pulled up to the new address on Stuart Road. A girl and two boys stood on the sidewalk across the street watching the movers lay out the ramp from the back of the huge van. Paul, Wade, and I tumbled out of the car ready to race inside and explore the new house while it was still empty. In minutes, dollies would roll down the ramp loaded with sofas and dressers, the washer and dryer, and fill up all those spaces. We knew the drill.

The scent in the air distracted me, very different from Syracuse. It must be the ocean. Mom had promised we could drive down to it tomorrow, after she had her kitchen put to rights.

The roar of a jet thundered overhead, a sound I hadn't heard since we lived in Niagara Falls. All three of us followed its ascent until it angled toward the sun. Once we returned our attention to earth, the girl from across the road was standing at my side.

"Hey, y'all." Her southern drawl caught my ear. As a general rule, Air Force kids never owned much of any accent since they moved around so much. But if a parent hailed from Alabama or Texas, their children grew up speaking "Southern" no matter what part of the country they lived in.

"Hi," I croaked. It didn't matter how many times we moved. As soon as I met a possible new friend, my hands got sweaty, my mind went blank, and I got all tongue-tied.

The six of us lined up in the driveway, facing each other in two matching trios. Me, Paul, and Wade across from the southern belle and two boys who looked about the same age as my brothers. Except for a difference in size, the new boys looked exactly alike with their sandy brown crewcuts and matching T-shirts and shorts. The smaller boy wore thick glasses magnifying his gray eyes, and his bony knees sported large scabs.

"Well, I'm Nancy, and these two here are Bradley and Michael." She gave the littler guy a Dutch rub on the top of his head. "We have a contest goin' on. Whoever gets the most points wins free ice cream from the Good Humor Man. The other two will pay."

Wade was a sucker for anything that involved free ice cream. "Can we join the contest too?"

Nancy shook her head and grinned, displaying large, straight, perfectly white teeth. "You *are* the contest."

Her brothers bobbed their heads in agreement.

With that confusing response, Wade ducked behind me like I was some kind of protective wall.

Nancy laughed. "Don't worry. It doesn't hurt to *be* the contest. Here's how it works. I get a point if a girl moves in, and I get a point for anyone who's my age. And Bradley gets a point if a boy moves in, and another point for anyone his age. And Michael gets a point if there's *another* boy who moves in, and for anyone *his* age."

That didn't sound like a fair contest for Michael.

Paul brought me back to the math problem at hand. "So you each get one point because there's one girl and two boys."

"Yeah." Nancy pointed at me. "What grade are you in?"

"I'm going into the sixth grade," I answered, eyeing her for a moment.

She slapped the taller boy on the shoulder, hard. "I told you she looked to be my size. I've got two points now."

Not to be outdone, the bigger brother—Bradley— eyed Paul. "So what grade are *you* goin' into?"

"I'm going into the fourth grade, and Wade'll be in the second." Paul often spoke for Wade without giving him a chance to say something for himself.

The three across from us broke into some kind of hootenanny. They jumped up and down and whooped like the Indians on *Wagon Train,* and they slapped each other on the back.

Paul interrupted their crazy celebration. "So, who won the bet?"

"We all did!" Nancy grabbed her brothers in a three-way hug.

"But that means nobody pays for anybody's ice cream," Wade pointed out. His sorrowful face caused the rest of us to bust out laughing.

"Who cares?" Nancy flipped the blond hair off her shoulder with a toss of her head. "We all got what we wanted."

Truer than she knew. I said goodbye to Francie two days ago, and now I'd met Nancy. Weird how both names rhymed. My first five minutes in Hampton Shores, and I already had a new friend.

"I'm Debbie," I said, nodding in the direction of our new house. "You want to come inside and explore with us?"

"If it's okay with your mom, it's okay with me."

"She won't care unless we get in the way of the moving men."

A loud screech from the van lassoed our attention. One of the men opened the side doors while Daddy and two other guys talked and gestured on the front lawn. As if on signal, all six of us ran for the front door. No time to lose.

"Bedrooms first!" Paul yelled. "Boys get the biggest."

"Mom and Dad get the biggest!" I shouted after him.

"That's what I meant. Boys get the next biggest."

I didn't bother to tell him that wasn't the case either. I already knew my room would be the next biggest. It would hold the crib and diaper-changing table along with two twin beds and my dresser.

Mom stepped from the kitchen into the front hall as we raced by, our pounding footsteps echoing in the emptiness of the place.

Still on the move, I called out, "Nancy and Bradley and Michael live across the street." Then I followed Paul and Wade, but somehow, I lost Nancy and her brothers. I turned back and saw all three had stopped, and there was Nancy shaking hands with my mother. The pleased expression on Mom's face told me she appreciated southern manners.

I checked out this new friend carefully since she wasn't looking in my direction. With the long, blond hair and blue eyes, we appeared similar, but Nancy was slender, a sleek greyhound compared to my beagle build. It had been kind of her to tell her brother that we looked to be the same size.

Nancy showed her mouthful of a white smile to Mom. "And my mother says for y'all to come on over whenever you get hungry. She has a whole lunch ready—baloney sandwiches, chicken salad, lots of fruits, and she even baked chocolate chip cookies."

My mouth watered, but breakfast had been less than an hour ago at a waffle place.

"Thank you," Mom said, grinning back at Nancy. "You tell her we'll be sure to come over."

I walked back to where they stood. "Is it okay if we explore the empty rooms before they all fill up?"

"Sure." Mom glanced toward the open front door. "And once the men get going, you kids stay outside. It's a beautiful day. We'll try to get your bikes off the van as soon as possible."

Nancy grabbed my arm. "Yeah, we'll ride all over base housing and show y'all everything!"

We started around the corner. "I'm pretty sure I know which room will be mine."

"The room at the end of the hall," Mom called from behind us. "Boys are on the left."

I breathed in the scent of freshly waxed floors as our sandals slapped out a rhythm on the bare wood. Door One on the left. A small room painted blue. The boys' bunkbeds would fit easily. Door Two on the left: bathroom. Door on the right: Mom and Dad's bedroom, and the only room with an extra phone jack, I'd bet.

Door at the end: mine. Actually, my *sister's* and mine. I'd never shared a room before. My brothers had been together all of their lives. Which was why it always seemed to be two against one between them and me. In a couple of years, I would finally have an ally.

My room was a nice size, painted a pale yellow. I'd wished for lavender walls, but the Air Force never paints a room that color.

Nancy turned in a circle. "This room is huge. How did your dad rate a stand-alone house while we have to live in a duplex? They're both captains, right?"

"How did you know my dad is a captain?"

"The name plate's already on the door." She stepped into the closet. "This is twice the size of mine."

"Maybe we get more space because I'll have to share my room soon."

Nancy giggled. "I noticed your mom's expecting." She nodded. "Yeah, that's probably it. I don't have to share my room."

A loud *thunk* sounded from the front of the house.

"I think the furniture is starting to come in." I stepped toward the door. "We'd better get out of the way."

Before we could leave the room, one of the men entered with metal bedrails. We slipped into the closet as he dropped them with a clatter. As soon as he left, Nancy stretched a finger toward the orange sticker on one of the rails.

I shooed her hand away. "Unh-uh. We have our own competition on moving day. That sticker is mine."

Every time we moved into a new house, Paul, Wade, and I raced to see who could find the most moving van stickers on the furniture. We peeled them off and stuck them all over our arms and legs, and if we ran out of space, we stuck them on our faces.

"You do that, too?" Her face took on joyful amazement.

We even played the same games. First, Francie. Now, Nancy. Two of the best friends ever.

Nancy skipped out the door, but I stopped to consider the almost-empty room soon to be filled with familiar possessions. What was Francie doing right now? Probably staring at the empty house behind hers thinking about the people who used to live there. She didn't have any girls her age in that neighborhood anymore. Poor Francie. Maybe the people who bought our old house had a kid going into sixth grade.

"You coming?" Nancy popped back into the room. "Your bike is out of the truck."

With a wistful, silent *Goodbye, Francie*, I followed my new friend. "Let's go."

Chapter 6:
Birth Day (September 21, 1965)

My house pushes me.
My mouth opens in protest.
I do not like this.

The aroma of brewed coffee woke me like it did every morning. A newscast on low volume floated from the radio, and a spoon clinked against glass as I ambled into the kitchen for breakfast. But it was our next-door neighbor, not Mom, who stood at the counter sipping from a coffee mug. Her presence could only mean one thing.

"The baby's coming?"

Mrs. Gaston smiled and nodded.

"They never woke me up. They promised!"

Mrs. Gaston patted my shoulder, but I jerked away. "Why, Debbie, what would you have done if they woke you at four in the morning?" Apparently, she wasn't fazed in the slightest by my grumpy attitude.

"Nothing." Tears filled my eyes, which only made me angrier. This was the most important day of my life, and my mom had lied to me. I stood as stiff as a mannequin when Mrs. Gaston placed an arm around me. Even with her sour coffee breath, it would be rude to jerk away, again. Her shiny, red-lacquered nails, bright against the sleeve of my white nightgown, served as another reminder that my mother wasn't home. Mom used *clear* nail polish. I tried to blink away the tears, but they spilled down my cheeks anyway.

"Oh, sweetie, it's an exciting day. I think you're a bit overwhelmed." Shiny red nails patted my cheek. "But you got your wish. The baby came in time for your birthday next week." She turned me around to face the hall. "Go get dressed for school. You'll feel better, and I'll have some breakfast for you in a jiff."

When I returned to the kitchen, the boys were chomping down on cold cereal. I wasn't hungry.

"Can we stay home today and wait for Dad to call?" Wade asked.

Mrs. Gaston tapped him on the head with her knuckles. "Not a chance, buddy. The day will go much faster at school."

Paul rinsed his green plastic bowl under the full force of the faucet. "Yeah, we could be waiting a long time sitting around here. Besides, I don't want to miss gym class."

I hated to admit it, but Paul was right. Some babies take all day to get born. What would I do here? Watch TV all day? Read a book for eight hours straight? That would be a stretch, even for me. Time would go faster at school.

As soon as the driver opened the door, I shot out of the bus, into cool September sunshine, and raced down the block, not even waiting for Nancy. I'd never outrun my brothers before. A couple of minutes later, I burst into the kitchen, chest heaving, and wind-tangled hair plastered to my face.

Daddy stood at the sink holding a sudsy plate. A dish towel matching the color of his light blue eyes was slung over his shoulder.

I gulped for air and rested my hands on my bent knees. "Boy or girl?" I asked in a wheezy gasp.

For months, I'd been sure baby *Krista* would arrive. I even prayed for her. What if God said no? What if I ended up with three little brothers, Paul, Wade, and--Patrick? *Patrick* would not be a welcome birthday present. Pat Hansen. Paddy Hansen. Stupid.

Daddy wore a sly, amused grin.

"Your mother ... gave birth ... to ... a little ..." He added the plate to a row of others on the drainboard.

"Dad-deeeee!" This was not the time for torture by procrastination.

"Girl." He said it so fast I almost missed it.

"A girl?" I whispered. "I have a sister?"

He nodded, the twinkle in his eyes unmistakable.

Joy bubbles fizzed through me, more and more of them, until I exploded like a shaken bottle of soda pop. "I have a sister! I have a Krista!" A crazy dance version of The Pony accompanied my screams of exultation.

Paul and Wade strolled into the house in the middle of my performance. Paul folded his arms across his chest. "I guess Mom had the baby."

"Yeah." Wade crossed his arms, too. "And I guess it's a girl."

"Yeah, a girl." You'd think Paul had found out he'd lost recess for a month, but then he hooked his arm around Wade's neck and anointed him with a vigorous Dutch rub. Oh, yeah, he was excited, too.

My wild dance screeched to a halt. After all the warnings that the baby wouldn't be normal, might not even live, Daddy hadn't said if she was okay.

I spun to face him, again, questions tumbling out of my mouth at breakneck speed. "How is she? Have the doctors found anything wrong? How much does she weigh? And how---"

"Whoa." Daddy raised his arms in self-defense. "One question at a time."

He slid one hand over his crew cut, then grasped the back of his neck. The shadows under his eyes reminded me of how I look when I get sick. Were the problems with the baby pretty bad, or was he just exhausted from being up most of the night and all day?

"Krista was born at high noon. She weighs six pounds, thirteen ounces, and she's eighteen inches long." Daddy picked up Wade's fire truck parked along the kitchen wall and held it in front of the boys. "About this long." He set the truck against the wall again. "So far, the doctor has noticed a heart murmur, but otherwise she seems healthy."

"I had a heart murmur," Wade said. "I guess that's not so bad."

Yeah, but your heart murmur didn't come from German measles, I wanted to say. "What about everything the doctors said would be wrong with her?"

"We have to wait and see. It's too early to tell about a lot of things." He laid the damp dish towel flat on the counter to dry. "I'm going to the hospital for a couple of hours, and then I'll be back to make dinner. You boys change into play clothes and go over to Mark and Paul's house. Their mom knows you're coming."

Paul and Wade galloped down the hall to their bedroom, giving each other little cuffs and kicks all the way.

"Debbie, do you want to go to Nancy's house or stay here?"

Oh, my gosh. I forgot all about her.

"I have to go over and tell her the news. I've already made her wait too long."

Chapter 7:
Heart Problems

Where are my fingers?
I've lost them! Too bright, too bright.
Shut my eyes and cry.

I didn't bother to wear a jacket to run across the street. Once we got into the privacy of her room, I held a hairbrush to my mouth like a microphone to make the big announcement. "I have… a *sister!*"

Nancy hollered a Texas hallelujah and grabbed my hands. We bounced around her room like we were on pogo sticks.

"You have a sister. You. Are. So. Lucky." She plopped onto the bed, flat on her back against the cowgirl-print bedspread, causing the stuffed blue poodle to jiggle on the pillow. "And I'm still stuck with two brothers."

I almost started twirling around the room again but limited myself to little hops from one foot to the other.

"When do you get to see her?" Nancy asked.

"Not till she and Mom come home. Maybe in two

or three days. I wish we could go to the hospital with my dad." I frowned. "I don't see why kids under thirteen can't visit."

"Can you picture my brothers in a hospital?" She rolled her eyes. "Brad would prob'ly jump on one of those beds with wheels and go flyin' into an operatin' room."

"He wouldn't be *that* bad." I kept hopping up and down. "I don't know what to do with myself. I can't stay still."

"That's a first."

For all of her energy, Nancy and I usually did quiet stuff. We'd get out our Barbie dolls or play a board game or just talk. We even spent hours sitting side by side, each reading her own book, but not on Krista's birthday.

"Let's ride bikes," I suggested.

"Mine's got two flat tires, remember?"

I groaned. "I don't know what to *do*." I stretched out the *oo* sound.

"I know." Nancy hopped off the bed and searched through a stack of forty-fives in her closet. "Here we go."

"What?"

"We're going to play records really loud and dance."

I was already dancing. "And we'll sing at the top of our lungs."

Nancy laughed. "And we can scream and howl, too, just like our dads do at beach parties."

She placed the stack on the thick spindle and slid the mechanism to release the first record. Familiar Beatles music filled the room as she turned the volume knob to the loudest it would go.

We danced. We stomped. We howled. "I'll never dance with another. *Owooooo*." Nancy's mom peeked in the open doorway. I waved. She waved back, smiled, and then closed the door.

After a tasteless dinner of macaroni and cheese—Daddy didn't make it right, too watery--I cleaned the kitchen while the boys watched television. Most nights, Paul moved the plates from the table to the counter, and Mom and I traded off on rinsing and washing dishes. Wade didn't have any chores involving food. He was going on eight years old and still spilled almost everything he put his hands on.

Nobody else noticed that Paul hadn't removed the plates, so I did it all—stacked them, rinsed them, washed them, and dried them—and I hated that last chore. For the whole time, Daddy sat at the table reading a bunch of papers from the hospital.

As I hung the wet dish towel over the oven handle like Mom always does, Daddy tapped the pile of papers into a neat stack, then slipped them into a folder. His eyebrows rose when he saw the empty sink and clean counter. "Wow, Debbie, nice job." The chair scraped against the floor as he got up from the table and hugged me. "You know, Mom will need your help around here for a little while."

I nodded. Though I despised housework, having all the responsibility while Mom was in the hospital kind of changed my feelings. Now, if I didn't help, chores would never get done.

"Can I go with you to the hospital tonight? They might let me in. I'm not noisy, and I don't break things." I offered him my sweetest *Daddy's Little Princess* smile.

He shook his head. "I'd like to take you, but rules are rules. The fewer the visitors, the fewer the germs, and I guess hospitals figure kids are germ factories."

I pointed to the sink where I had just slaved for an hour. "I have the cleanest hands on the base right now, and if I put on a little makeup, I'd look older. Maybe even as old as fourteen."

His eyes widened. "Ha! Makeup, my foot."

Whenever Daddy used *my foot* in a sentence, he'd never change his mind. I might be Daddy's princess, but I sure couldn't wrap him around my little finger. I marched out of the kitchen and down the hall into my room. So that was the thanks I got for cleaning the whole, entire kitchen by myself.

Daddy gave me my two-minute cooling-off period, then appeared in my doorway. "Still mad?"

As I sat cross-legged on my bed, I stared at the flowers on my bedspread and refused to answer. Big mistake.

He strode across the room, stuck his face smack in front of mine, and crossed his eyes. I struggled to hold on to my frown.

In a deep, basso voice he announced, "This looks like a job for—Tickle Man."

I scrambled off the bed and backed into the corner of the diaper-changing table. Ouch. "No tickling. See my smile? I'm not pouting anymore."

He peered into my face again. "Let's make sure." He poked my ribs.

I darted away, giggling. I could never stay mad at him for longer than ten minutes, anyhow.

He called the boys into my room. "Everybody in pajamas by the time I get home. I'll be back in about two hours. Call Mrs. Gaston if there's a problem. You can each have a glass of juice, no snacks, and Wade keeps his juice in the kitchen. Any questions?"

We stood in a line like three soldiers. "Nope," we said in unison. Wade and Paul saluted.

Daddy chuckled. "Okay. See you in a bit."

Everything ran smoothly while he was gone. Wade spilled his juice in the kitchen, and he helped me clean it up. When Daddy got home, we were all ready for bed. We even brushed our teeth without anybody telling us to.

His favorite jazz tunes floated from the hi-fi in the living room when he came to tuck me in. I sat up in bed and asked again how Krista was doing.

He sighed. "She has some problems, but I think she'll be all right."

I twisted the silky sheet around my fingers creating a cocoon for my hand. "More problems than a heart murmur?" My voice could barely whisper.

Daddy stared at me for a moment. The look on his face reminded me of the time I'd asked if I could ride my bike across the highway to the ice cream shop. He nodded his head with a sigh. "Yes, the baby has more problems than a heart murmur."

"What are they?" *My* heart started thumping hard.

In the soft light of the bedside table, Daddy looked more solemn than I'd ever seen him. "Debbie, your mom thinks we shouldn't tell you everything, but I believe you're capable of handling the situation."

I swallowed and pressed my lips together, ready for whatever would hit me, and I looked directly into his eyes. If he thought I was old enough to know the facts, then I would face them head-on, no matter how much I wanted to hide under the covers. *Don't cry. Don't cry,* I reminded myself.

"Right now, we know of two problems Krista has to overcome. The doctors found a cataract on her right eye. It looks like a white cloud covering the pupil, the black part." He took another deep breath. "Chances are she can't see out of that eye, and it'll need an operation to remove the cataract." He peered into my eyes and paused for a minute to let his words sink in.

I chewed on my bottom lip, refusing to allow anxious thoughts to overwhelm me. A cataract sounded alarming but fixable. At least Krista still had one good eye.

He continued, apparently satisfied that I wasn't going to get hysterical over the news. "And she has more than a heart murmur." Ominous silence. "Krista… has a hole in her heart. The leak is what's causing the heart murmur." He sighed for a third time as he sat down on my bed. "It's a serious situation. Even though heart surgery is dangerous, she'll need an operation as soon as possible."

I'd learned in science that the heart is about the most important part of your entire body. It pumps blood to every area. If it doesn't… My mouth went dry, and my mind refused to finish that thought. I could barely get the next question out over the lump in my throat. "Will… will Krista die?"

He gently tugged the bunched-up part of the sheet from my fist and smoothed it out. "If the operation goes well, she'll be fine."

He hadn't answered my question with a solid *no*. The lump grew bigger, but I asked another question despite it. "When will they do the surgery?"

He shrugged. "I don't know. They'll wait for her to grow and get stronger. She can live with her heart this way for a little while."

I lay back against my pillow. The baby wasn't in immediate danger. I could squeeze some relief from that knowledge.

Daddy leaned over me. "Are you okay?"

I nodded. "Yes."

"You sure?"

The fact that I wasn't crying should let him know I was telling the truth. I hunched my shoulders and offered him a small, close-lipped smile. "Yeah. It's just… a lot to think about."

He kissed my cheek. The stubble on his face and the hint of aftershave and perspiration comforted me. He turned out the light, and I was left alone to think. Ever since Mom told me the new baby might have problems, I'd talked to God about Krista more than anything else in my whole life. So far, He'd answered one prayer with a *yes*. The baby wasn't blind. Only *half* blind. So, I would keep talking to God about this until He made sure the doctors fixed Krista's heart, too.

I closed my eyes and began a list of rhyming words, something I often did until I bored myself to sleep. *Ab, cab, dab, gab, jab, lab*—but my whirring brain interrupted. Mom had already held her new baby. She must be more worried than I was. I hadn't even seen Krista yet, and I was plenty worried. *Nab, tab…* onto *ebs: Deb, ebb, Jeb*—was Mom struggling to fall asleep like I was? I gave up on the rhyme list, scrunched my eyelids tighter, and prayed, not only for Krista, but for our whole family. We needed God's help more than ever before.

Chapter 8:
Meeting Krista

Wrapped in soft layers,
I peek out at this new world.
Cold air blasts my face.

Daddy planned to get Mom and Krista right after lunch. My first birthday present had arrived three days early.

"Why can't we go, too?" Wade sat at the kitchen table with his eyes on the thick layer of strawberry jam spread on the slice of bread in front of him. "We'll wait in the car until you come back with Mom."

"Not a good idea." Daddy swirled the knife in the jar of peanut butter, bringing up a glob to spread on slices of bread.

Careful not to knock over my glass of milk, I leaned over the open jar to breathe in the mix of salt, peanuts, and oil.

Paul gave a two-fingered Cub Scout salute. "We promise we won't fight. I'll even bring a book to read."

Daddy grinned. "Nice try, but I don't know how

long it will take to get everything packed and the baby bundled up. You can't stay in the car for hours."

He slapped peanut butter slices against jelly slices and handed each of us a sandwich. "Just think of the pandemonium once we got in the car. You three would be a deluge of noise and scare the baby to death. Nope. Better for you to stay here and wait."

I knew what pandemonium was. My brothers caused a lot of it. But deluge? How could loud voices and a hundred hugs make a flood? I pictured me, Paul, and Wade exploding out of the car and rushing toward Mom with babe in arms, knocking them down like a breaking wave in the ocean. Guess that could be a deluge.

A knock on the door interrupted our argument. Mrs. Gaston had arrived from next door. Her short, dark hair stuck up in spikes after running across the yard in the rain and wind. Daddy had told me this morning we were too excited to stay home alone and couldn't be trusted to take care of ourselves—as if we were toddlers. With a quick "see you later," he grabbed his coat and umbrella and was gone.

Since Mom went to the hospital, it felt more like two whole weeks instead of four days. I used to think I'd be glad *not* to see her for a week or two so I wouldn't have to hear, "Debbie, pick up your room," or "Debbie, please dust the living room," or "Debbie, stop reading and go outside."

The past few days had been more than enough time without Mom, and I missed telling her all about school every afternoon. Talking to Nancy's mother wasn't the same at all. I missed homemade desserts. Daddy only served canned peaches or ice cream. Nothing special.

Just plain old vanilla.

I was losing things, too, and only Mom could ever find the stuff we needed--like my purple headband. How could I pull it off of my head before taking a bath and lose it? Or my sneakers. I thought I kicked them off while watching television, but I only found the left one under the couch. And after three days, none of my socks matched. Half of each pair must have run off and joined the missing sneaker. Once Mom got home, would she still be able to find all this stuff, or would she be too busy with the new baby?

A crash from the living room followed by an abrupt silence rousted me out of my worries and sent Mrs. Gaston running. She had been trying to wash up lunch dishes, and her hands dripped water all over the floor. Curious as to what broke, I pushed out of my chair and joined Mrs. Gaston's investigation.

Dad's chessboard. Somehow, one of the boys had sent the entire board flying across the room. Paul picked it up and carried it back to the coffee table in front of the couch. Wade was chasing down a pawn that still rolled its way to the dining room.

"Pick up this mess right now," Mrs. Gaston demanded. Her eyebrows joined a wrinkle right above her nose.

"That's what we're doing." Paul retorted with more sass than he ever was allowed to show Mom.

"Your father treasures this chess set. It's very expensive. You could've broken it." Mrs. Gaston continued, as her hand perched on her hip and her red-nailed finger wagged at the boys.

"It's made of wood," Wade said. "Wood doesn't break like glass does."

Mrs. Gaston gave him a squinty-eyed stare, and he turned quickly, busying himself with collecting more chess pieces.

"When you're done cleaning up, go outside and run around the house twenty-five times, and get some of this energy out of yourselves."

"In the rain?" Paul raised his eyebrows with interest. "Do we have to wear coats?"

Mrs. Gaston didn't crack a smile, but I could tell she was ready to laugh. "No."

"Neat." Paul joined Wade's search for missing chessmen with renewed energy.

They put the chess set back together, ran around the house coatless, and slid their way back inside, soaked and out of breath.

Mrs. Gaston handed them each a towel before they could step away from the front door. "Take off your muddy shoes and toss them in the garage. Then have a seat." She pointed to the kitchen table where hot chocolate waited for them. She didn't have to ask twice.

I didn't want hot chocolate. I didn't even want to read a book. All I wanted was for Mom, Daddy, and Krista to get home.

Any time I get this restless, I play song after song on the piano to forget whatever's bothering me. My fingertips pound on the keys, and I guess it's exactly the same feeling my brothers must have gotten from running around the house.

This time, though, playing the piano didn't work. After attempting one song, I jumped up to look out the window to see if our car was rolling down the road. Nope. So, back to the piano. I concentrated really hard on "Blue Spanish Eyes," a piece with tough rhythms and chords. No dice. I returned to the window and scanned the road for our car, again. Nothing. Then, back to the piano.

In the middle of "Moon River," the very last song in the book, I heard a whoop from Paul. "They're here! They're turning into the driveway."

All three of us crashed over each other trying to reach the kitchen door first.

Mrs. Gaston stepped in front of Paul, who won the race. She was taller than Mom, and her sharp features took on a witchy look. "Go back and sit at the table. Your mom is *not* strong enough to have three big kids like you bumping up against her to see the baby."

Daddy was right… we were definitely a deluge.

"You'll each get a turn to hold the baby, I'm sure." She stood with arms akimbo, blocking any moves toward the garage.

We could see around her; she was pretty skinny. Daddy helped Mom out of the car. She held a bundle of blankets in her arms. None of us wanted to move back to the table.

"Now," Mrs. Gaston ordered, pointing toward the table.

We shuffled to our directed space. The boys grabbed the two chairs closest to the middle of the room so they could be closer to the baby. I took a seat by the wall. Mom would surely let me hold the baby first. I was the oldest, and a girl.

Mrs. Gaston welcomed them inside. Mom's dark hair waved around her face, and her eyes sparkled. She smiled over at us, more beautiful than Elizabeth Taylor. Mrs. Gaston took the bundle of blankets so Daddy could help Mom off with her coat. She still wore a maternity top but looked a lot thinner than four days ago.

Mrs. Gaston carefully lifted the layers of blankets. "Oh, Dorothy, she's so sweet."

Paul, Wade, and I couldn't help it. We bounded out of our seats to deluge Mom and Mrs. Gaston. We hugged Mom, peeked at the baby, and hugged Mom again.

I couldn't tell much from one little peek. Krista was just a tiny round head covered with a thin layer of brown hair. As soon as we had gathered around her, she'd closed her eyes. Maybe our deluge scared her.

Daddy led Mom to the living room and helped her get comfortable in an easy chair. He treated her as if she'd bruise at any careless touch, like the delicate heroine in *The Princess and the Pea.*

Wade tried to sit on Mom's lap.

"No." Daddy grasped him by the shoulders and set him to one side. "You're too heavy for Mommy right now. Instead, you can stand next to the chair and lean on her shoulder."

Mrs. Gaston followed us into the living room. She had removed the heavy blankets and started to hand Krista back to Mom.

Mom shook her head. "We'll let each of the kids take a turn. They've been waiting for days to hold her."

Wade ran to the couch and sat between Paul and me. "Me first. Me first," he insisted.

"No. Me first." Paul jabbed an elbow into Wade's ribs. Wade ignored him and sat with hands folded like a blond angel.

I sat quietly, too, squeezing the arm of the sofa. I wanted to hold Krista so badly.

"I think Wade first, then Paul, then Debbie," Mom said.

Not fair. My jaw tightened, and I tried to keep my lips from trembling. Wade didn't know the first thing about holding babies. At least, I had some experience helping out in the church nursery. Though bitter jealousy bubbled in me like magma inside a volcano, I continued to sit up straight. I would not make a scene and blow my top as soon as Mom had gotten home.

Mrs. Gaston helped Wade hold the baby, placing his left arm under her head and his right hand supporting her back.

"Wow, she hardly weighs anything. I thought she'd be heavier." He peered down at her. "She doesn't have much hair." Satisfied with his inspection, he handed her off to Mrs. Gaston and scampered back to Mom.

Paul's turn. He held the baby like she might break. Her eyes opened, and she seemed to look past his shoulder. "I think she's going to have brown eyes like me," he announced. If he was right, things would be even. One boy and girl with blue eyes, and one boy and girl with brown eyes. Maybe he would have spent a little more time holding her, but the baby stretched her little legs and arms, and he hurriedly returned her to Mrs. Gaston, probably afraid he'd drop her, and then she *would* break.

Very gently, Mrs. Gaston placed Krista in my arms. The baby was easier to hold than I thought. My left arm supported her slight weight, and her perfect little head rested on the curve inside my elbow. So tiny. The Scottish would call her a *wee bairn.* I read that in a book once. She looked so cozy and comfortable tightly wrapped in a pink flannel blanket. The scent of newborn infant mixed with baby powder surrounded her.

Krista blinked and stared at the wall. My finger traced her silky cheek, and she shifted her gaze to my face, and *smiled.*

I gasped, my voice hushed. "Mom, look! She's smiling at me!"

"It's probably a little gas. Newborns can't smile yet."

I didn't argue. Krista had smiled at me. I knew she had.

Paul jumped off the couch. "C'mon, Wade. Let's play marbles." They ran down the hall toward their bedroom, feet pounding on the wood floor.

"Boys, quietly." Mom put a finger to her lips. "You'll startle the baby."

They slowed to a fast walk, trying to step lightly. Krista lay peacefully in my arms as if she hadn't heard a thing.

"See, Debbie?" Mom raised her eyebrows, with a slight grin. "Now you get to hold Krista for as long as you want."

Boy, did she know me or what? I hadn't said a word, I hadn't pouted, but she knew I was hurt when she let Wade hold the baby first.

I relaxed into the sofa cuddling Krista against me, this real, live, tiny, fragile infant. When I got married, I would have at least seven babies so I could hold them like this.

Krista continued to stare at my face. Her sweet curve of a smile showing now and again, She trusted me completely.

Chapter 9:
Sick Baby

Bottle in my mouth.
Too much food. Just let me sleep.
Kiss my cheek. I smile.

Another rainy Saturday. What a waste. What a waste of *eight* Saturdays. Eight all-day rains. I'd been counting. Paul and Wade had played their entire little league football season in the rain. Now that their games were over, Mom had decreed they wouldn't play football in the yard on *another* rainy day. She was tired of mud dragged into her house, which meant nobody went outside.

Paul aimed his trusty Lone Ranger pistol at Wade. "Stop, or I'll shoot!"

Startled by his bellow, I nearly jumped out of the easy chair. Good thing I wasn't the one holding Krista, or I might've dropped her. Nancy's brothers were even louder than mine, though, and she kept the baby tucked securely against her ribs.

Wade, with a feather stuck in *my* headband that

circled *his* head, tried to dodge Cowboy Paul by ducking behind the dining room table. No wonder Mom had never found that headband. Neither of us had thought to search the *boys'* bedroom.

Paul took aim. "*Bang.* You're dead!." His voice reverberated in my ears.

"Am not," Wade argued. "You can't shoot through this wall."

"I got you before you hid behind there." Paul holstered his gun. "Remember the Alamo! And all the Indians died at the Alamo. Right, Nancy?" He had a huge crush on her. Showing off was his way of impressing her.

She rolled her eyes and heaved a sigh. "There weren't any Indians at the Alamo. The Americans were fighting the Mexicans."

"Oh." Paul shifted his eyes away from his idol.

"And all the *Americans* died at the Alamo." She smiled innocently but was probably biting her tongue trying not to laugh. I choked back a snicker.

While Paul searched the floor for his dignity, Wade slid by with his makeshift hatchet and smacked him on the back. "Ha! Now *you're* dead."

Paul snared him by the collar and wrenched him backward. "You only wounded me. Prepare to die!" They fell to the ground, yelling, wrestling for Paul's gun, and rolled right into a dining room chair, flipping it over. The chair clattered to the wood floor.

Mom appeared from down the hall, her eyes flashing fire. "Boys!" She stomped over to Paul and Wade lying breathless on the floor. Wade's lip quivered, but he knew better than to start blubbering or blame Paul for everything. Mom never bought it.

She pulled them to their feet. "I've told you a dozen times. Be quiet or you'll wake the baby." Her voice was even louder than the boys' battle. *She'd* be the one who would end up waking the baby. My eyes met Nancy's. Yeah, she thought the same thing.

Mom pointed toward the bedrooms. "Paul, go to your room and lie down. Do absolutely nothing until I come in and tell you to get up. Wade, go sit on a kitchen chair. Don't. Move." She peered closely at Wade. "Is that my lipstick that you have striped all over your cheeks?"

His chin jerked one time in a nervous nod.

"Go wash it off. *Then* sit in the kitchen." She strode down the hall, back to folding laundry or rinsing out dirty diapers or something.

With everything quiet again, I gazed at Krista. Sound asleep, as usual. Not once had she stirred. I relaxed back into my chair and kept my gaze on her. There's nothing better than watching a sleeping infant.

Nancy shifted the baby to her other side, maybe to give her arm a rest. Krista breathed a sweet sigh but didn't open her eyes.

"I thought babies were wigglier than this." Nancy bent forward and kissed Krista's forehead.

I reached over and stroked the satin edge of Krista's blanket. "She's just a peaceful baby."

"I guess so." Nancy caressed Krista's cheek with her index finger. "Last year, when I held my baby cousin, he squirmed so much I was scared I'd drop him."

"Maybe girls aren't as squirmy as boys."

"Yeah, maybe."

It made me wonder, though. Mom used to say

Krista hardly ever moved inside her at all, not like the other three of us. Could something be wrong with her arms and legs? Was her damaged little heart working so hard that she had no energy to wiggle and stay awake?

Every couple of weeks, Mom took Krista to doctors to check her progress. And it was rarely good news. They weren't sure her kidneys worked right. Her heart murmur was worse. Kidneys were better, but she was too weak.

One piece of news was always the same: the baby needed to gain more weight.

Grandma said my parents shouldn't be telling us kids what the doctors reported, but Mom and Daddy wanted us to be prepared if something bad happened. What kind of bad should I prepare for? A sister in a wheelchair? A sister in heaven? I didn't think I could handle losing Krista to heaven.

Sometimes, Wade cried. Paul didn't say anything. I had no idea what he was thinking, but I sure knew the thoughts racing across my mind like a chaotic game of Red Rover.

Red Rover, Red Rover, let heart attack cross over. Except *all* the worries crossed over at the same time. *Let deafness cross over. Let lameness cross over. Let sickness cross over. Let slow brains cross over.* All I could do to stop the worries from breaking through the barrier was to hold on tight to Jesus' hand.

Should I do *more* than pray for Krista? I remembered what Daddy said before Krista was born. Difficult things aren't always bad. You make a plan to handle the storm.

As I watched Krista sleep in Nancy's arms, a plan began to form. I could show her how to move those arms and legs. Play Patty-cake. Kiss her toes so she would jerk away and giggle. I could check that she was still breathing every night when I went to bed. I could watch carefully to see how she reacted to sound. The boys' sharp noises from this afternoon sure didn't wake her. I could teach her letters and numbers and colors when she was old enough and see how quickly she learned.

God knew how to fix Krista, and I would do my part to help.

I sat at the kitchen table reading *A Wrinkle in Time*. I rarely read a book more than once, but I couldn't get enough of Meg's amazing adventure. This was my third go-round.

Mom walked in from the garage holding a bundled-up Krista. "Where are your brothers?" she asked in exasperation.

Not even a hello? "I think they're across the street."

She strode out of the kitchen and down the hall, probably to get Krista unbundled and into her crib. She was back shortly, jerking open drawers, grabbing silverware, and letting it all drop on the table with a crash. I almost tipped over my chair as I tried to scoot away from any sharp objects that might slide my way.

Mom pasted a bright smile on her face. "Dr. Arnold wants to operate on Krista's heart after the new year. He wants her to get up to ten pounds, and he thinks she should make it there by next month." She lifted a bunch of plates from their shelves and almost dropped *them* on the table.

Something was wrong. "How much did she weigh today?"

"Eight pounds, seven ounces." She set two pots on the stove. *Bang, bang.*

While she yanked vegetables out of the refrigerator and tossed them on the counter, I did the math in my head. At one month, Krista had weighed seven pounds, ten ounces, less than a pound over her birth weight. Now, at two months old she hadn't even reached eight and a half pounds. No, surgery would have to wait. Next month was less than two weeks away, and she couldn't make it to ten pounds that fast.

"But she hasn't gained two pounds since she was born." I dipped my celery stalk into the peanut butter jar. "How can she gain two more by December?"

Mom's fake, cheerful expression crumpled. "I don't think she'll gain that much either, but the doctor says he'll operate anyway." She paused from furiously slicing a tomato and wiped the tear rolling down her cheek. "The hole in her heart only makes her weaker each day. She can't get stronger until they sew it up."

The knife dropped from Mom's hand onto the cutting board with a *thud.* "Excuse me," she said in a shaky voice as she ran out of the kitchen, her footsteps echoing down the hall.

Tears dropped onto the pages of my book. Tears for my mom, whose heart was breaking and tears for my baby sister, who couldn't grow because her heart was already broken.

The aroma of fresh tomato filled the kitchen, sparking memories of summer, warmth, and life, but the knife looked like a murder weapon as it lay in the center of the sliced-up tomato.

Daddy's words from the night Krista was born flew around in my brain like a panicked fly trapped inside a lampshade. *Hole in her heart—dangerous surgery—hole in her heart—she can live for a little while—dangerous surgery.*

Live for a little while? Time was up.

Chapter 10:
To the Hospital

Mouths name a person.
Mah-mi, Da-di, Deh-bi, Paw,
Way. Me? *Oo-ihd-duh.*

I jiggled the bottle's nipple in Krista's mouth and coaxed her to drink more. With each sentence, my voice rose higher and higher, and so did my eyebrows, until I squeaked, and my eyebrows must have reached my hairline. "Come on, Krista. Come on, baby-baby. You can do it. Just a little bit more. An itsy-bitsy little bit more. An itsy-bitsy, teeny-weeny, little bit more."

Krista pushed the bottle out of her mouth with her little pink tongue and gave me her sweet, toothless smile. Not the response I was looking for. I set the bottle on the end table with a sigh and snuggled her against me. She loved to be held.

Since I wouldn't be holding her for a long time—that old stupid rule—no one under thirteen allowed in the hospital—I wanted to remember the feeling of her snuggled in my arms. Krista's heart operation was scheduled for January tenth. Her doctor said she would stay in the hospital a whole month, which made me wish Christmas vacation would last forever.

I rested my cheek against the top of her head with its silky hair and breathed in the baby smell of her. My lips pressed to her forehead, and I sniffed back a sob. Her eyes fluttered closed, and just like that, she was asleep again. So peaceful.

I wished I could have that kind of peace. Instead, I worried. I didn't fret about whether she'd survive the operation. God was in control of that, and He didn't give me a little sister just to take her away. No, I worried about how scared Krista would be in a strange place with strange people.

Hospitals. Horrible places. When I was five, I had my tonsils out and had to stay overnight in the army hospital at Fort Knox. The room was drab and ugly and smelled like my mom had mopped the floor with ammonia. Doctors and nurses made me choke down pills and stuck thermometers in my mouth—or other places. Back then, there'd been nothing wrong with me except for tonsils that kept getting infected. *My* heart was fine, not like my sister's.

Would the operation hurt her terribly? I couldn't stand the thought of Krista in pain. Not only from the surgery. She would get lots of shots. I was twelve and still hated shots.

Would she be lonely? Only Mom would be with her, and not all the time. Would the nurses take time to play with her? Would she *want* strangers trying to play with her? Would she be able to play at *all* after such a serious operation?

Would she forget me in a month? I read that babies

don't have long memories.

Would Krista die? She was so little. She'd made it to nine pounds, but no farther. Mom and Daddy were worried. They hadn't said anything to me, but I'd discovered if I put my ear on the wall between our bedrooms, I could hear most of what they talked about. So I learned this open-heart surgery was pretty new, especially on children, and Krista might be the smallest patient the surgeon had ever operated on. Doctors said Krista would only get weaker and weaker until she died if she didn't have the operation. The light from my sparkly baby sister would slowly dim until it winked out.

No! That was *not* going to happen.

But I was also scared about her staying in the hospital for an entire month. If I could barely survive one, single night, how could she stay alive in a place like that for so long?

The doctor said he could fix her heart with this new surgery. He'd better be right.

By New Year' s Day, nerves were stretched to the breaking point like strings wound too tight on a guitar. The boys fought about everything, I cried over everything, and Mom yelled at all of us, whether we deserved it or not. Krista must have sensed our moods, and for the first time in her life, she became a fussy baby, which did nothing for Mom's temper. Only Daddy remained calm. He soothed the baby, listened to my woes, refereed my brothers' fights, and hugged Mom, even when she yelled at *him.*

Krista, Mom, and Daddy left for the hospital on January seventh. When I'd asked why she had to go there three days early, Mom said there were lots of tests to do and some kind of *observation.*

I stood in the doorway of my bedroom, still in my pajamas, and silently watched as Mom changed Krista and bundled her in blankets. A vinyl bag sat on the floor crammed with baby powder, wash cloths, extra sets of clothes, and the newfangled disposable diapers. No cloth diapers at the hospital.

How could I walk in here later today? The safe haven of my bedroom would become a torture chamber, the crib relentlessly beating me with the fact that it was empty.

"It looks like Krista's moving away." My voice caught in my throat. "Like the diaper bag is her suitcase."

Mom didn't look up, but her jaw tightened as she pulled snug one last blanket around Krista. "Pretend she's going to camp like you do every summer." She turned to me and tried to smile.

I couldn't play along. I never went to camp for more than two weeks. Krista would be gone a lot longer, but I didn't want to make Mom feel worse by pointing that out.

She hoisted Krista to her shoulder. "Would you take the bag to Daddy, please?" She moved past me through the doorway and didn't look back. I trudged after her, diaper bag in hand.

Paul and Wade sat in the kitchen, silent, pushing cereal around with their spoons and pretending to eat it. I handed the bag to Daddy. With a quiet "thank you," he stepped outside to put it in the car. When he came back in, Mom handed Krista to me while she allowed Daddy to help her with her coat.

She leaned over the table and kissed each of the boys. She wrapped her arms around me, pulled me close, and kissed the top of my head. "It will be all right, sweetie. Don't cry."

Which only made the tears fall faster.

She stepped away. "Be good."

Daddy reached for the baby.

I looked down at Krista, who peeked out from all her wrappings and offered me a grin. I smiled back. I rolled her in closer to me and caught a whiff of her. My eyes welled with tears, and I refused to hand over my warm bundle to Daddy.

"Debbie." His voice was gentle but firm. He didn't need to say anything more.

He took Krista from me, and though I trembled when she left my embrace, my arms didn't resist.

Chapter 11:
Heart Surgery

*Why is there so much
Pain? Screaming hurts. Hiccups hurt.
Mah-mi strokes my cheek.*

Isn't Inger Stevens beautiful?" Nancy smiled dreamily as the credits rolled on *The Farmer's Daughter*. Monday night TV.

"Yeah."

Yesterday, I would have said something like, "You're gonna be just as beautiful." Nancy, slender and blond, would probably look like the gorgeous Swedish actress someday, but my mind wasn't on Hollywood movie stars.

A potato chip jingle replaced *The Farmer's Daughter* theme music. Nancy scooped another handful of popcorn from the yellow plastic bowl that sat between us on the McKenzies' plush velour sofa. The buttery aroma smothered the last stink of cooked cabbage from dinner, which I couldn't have choked down if someone had ordered me to eat it at gunpoint.

Nancy dropped a kernel and winced as it landed between the cushions. Even though she snatched it up again, a small grease stain had formed. We'd broken a lot of house rules tonight since everyone felt sorry for poor Debbie whose sister was in the hospital.

Krista had her heart operation this morning, so Mom and Daddy decided to stay at the hospital all night. Which meant Paul, Wade, and I stayed at different places. Of course, I was at Nancy's house.

Did Krista wake up yet? Was she hurting? Could they give tiny babies pain medicine?

Other than Daddy's one phone call to tell us the operation went well, I hadn't heard anything more.

At ten, *Ben Casey* came on.

"What a dreamboat!" Nancy was in TV heaven being allowed to stay up so late on a school night and watch Vince Edwards play the perfect doctor. She wiggled her toes that were snuggled in crazy dinosaur socks.

I ought to have been as excited. A pajama party on a school night, and we didn't have to put up with her brothers' disgusting sound effects. They had to go to bed at the regular time. We wore our almost matching flannel nightgowns, Nancy in hot pink and me in pale pink. Not only were we allowed to stay up, even better for me, the McKenzies' console television had a screen tons bigger than ours.

I *wasn't* excited, though. Sensible, white cotton socks suited *my* mood. Ben Casey the Dreamboat didn't interest me. I just wondered what Ben Casey the Doctor would do with a patient like Krista. Her surgery would be a guaranteed success if *he* operated. But real life didn't always work out like what happened on make-believe television shows.

I rubbed the soft, worn flannel between two fingers and dozed off. When I woke up, doctors were mumbling over some patient on the operating table, which only made me think of helpless little Krista lying there. Maybe a handful of popcorn would replace the stale taste of worry in my mouth. But Nancy had helped herself to the whole bowl.

I wasn't hungry anyway.

Mom scooped vanilla ice cream for Tuesday night's dessert and poured butterscotch sauce all over the double mounds in each bowl. She gave Daddy *three* scoops.

He had taken a seat at the kitchen table and was sketching the outline of a man on a sheet of notebook paper. Paul, Wade, and I watched the drawing develop, none of us speaking a word. Inside the man's chest, Daddy drew a diagram of the human heart. It looked more like a tree trunk and several bare branches. Those were supposed to be blood vessels.

"It turns out the hole wasn't in Krista's heart, but in the aorta, the biggest blood vessel in your whole body." He pointed to something that had two parallel lines, like a thick tree trunk, stretching out from the heart and down toward the belly. "Krista's aorta was leaking."

He added a hole to the tree trunk.

That looked just as bad as if it had been in the heart itself. The tree trunk lines were so wide apart, I hadn't realized it *was* one of the blood vessels.

Daddy continued the lesson. "The aorta carries a lot of blood. Luckily, the hole was very tiny, but even losing a little blood in a baby is harmful. That's why Krista wasn't growing fast."

Paul put his pointer finger on the outline's aorta. "How did the doctor get in there to sew it up?" He pressed a fist against his ribs. "All of those squishy parts inside of us are covered by bones."

As Mom handed around the bowls of ice cream, she and Daddy exchanged an amused smile.

"Squishy parts?" Daddy asked.

"Yeah, the heart, the liver, the stomach. There's a bunch of others, too. We watched a filmstrip in health class."

The horror in Mom's voice matched the expression on her face. "They showed you photos of real hearts in health class? You're only in fourth grade!"

"No," he scoffed. "The filmstrip just showed drawings. Better than Dad's."

Daddy threw him a fake glare, and Paul snorted a laugh.

Mom continued to fish for the culprit who exposed her little boy to the grossness of our insides. "So how do you know hearts and livers are squishy?"

"I watch you cook the turkey every Thanksgiving." He raised his hands in a confused, what's-the-problem-here gesture. "You pull the guts out of the turkey, put 'em in a pot, and make gravy. You always show me the liver and the heart and the gizzard. They're squishy."

Daddy clapped a hand over his mouth so he wouldn't spit out melted ice cream. Once he managed to swallow, he grinned at Mom. "No one to blame for the over-education of your son, my dear, except yourself."

"You're terrible." She stole a spoonful of ice cream from his bowl and gave him a butterscotch smooch.

"So how did the doctor get inside there to sew up her heart?" Paul still waited for an answer to his question as his spoon clinked against the empty bowl.

"Oh." Dad returned to his drawing. "The surgeon made an incision—a cut—from the center of her chest, around her left side, and almost halfway across her back to the wing bone."

He pulled Wade to his feet, who giggled from tickles as Daddy's finger skimmed around his ribs from front to back.

I hugged my own ribs as if to protect them. "You mean the doctor had to cut Krista almost in half?"

Mom sucked in a sharp breath. Daddy's hand dropped.

Wade's laugh disappeared. "The doctor could have killed her!" He pointed an accusing finger at Daddy, and his eyes filled with tears.

Daddy drew several little x's part way around the outline's middle before he lifted his gaze to meet mine. "Every operation on our squishy parts, as Paul so accurately puts it, requires the surgeon to slice into the body. When you think about it, it's hideous."

He tapped the outline with his pencil. "But people in medicine have learned how to do it without killing the patient. So don't look at the doctor as if he were a criminal, Debbie. Wade." He glanced across the table at my brothers. "Instead, thank God that we live at a time when man has learned to do the miraculous. Dr. Arnold saved Krista's life."

I stared into my lap and shook my head. "I know that, but… it looks like it hurts. A lot." I tried to hold back the tears. "How can Krista stand it?"

"They've given her medicine for the pain," Mom assured me. "And the same medicine helps her to sleep a lot."

"Which is why both of us came home tonight," Daddy added. "Once we knew she was out of danger, we decided to get a good night's sleep ourselves."

If Krista was sleeping right this minute, then she wasn't in pain.

The cold spoon clicked against my teeth while smooth ice cream slid down my throat.

Wade put the bowl to his lips and slurped the last of his melted ice cream. After wiping his mouth with the back of his hand, he said, "When will Krista be better enough to come home?"

Mom stacked the empty bowls while Daddy answered. "Assuming she heals according to the doctor's schedule, she can leave the hospital in three weeks."

The kitchen clock ticked away on the wall beside me. How many tick-tocks before Krista could come home?

That was the last report of any kind about Krista. Ever since, I didn't know if the doctors stopped giving her pain medicine or not. I didn't know if she had happy moments or if she was always unhappy. I didn't know *anything*. The most Mom ever said was that the baby cried often and wouldn't eat.

"To be expected," she assured me and the boys with a tired smile.

Mom left home every morning right after the school bus picked us up. Some days she followed the bus out of the neighborhood. She returned once Krista was asleep for the night. I was usually still awake after her two-hour drive, but not the boys. On Sundays, she didn't go to the hospital until after church, and she came home for dinner. She probably needed a break.

Exactly one week after Krista's surgery, Mom came home looking more relaxed than usual. She entered the living room where Daddy and I had been reading, and the boys were watching cartoons filled with a lot of banging and crashes.

She smiled. "Guess what?"

"What?" I asked.

"Krista learned how to suck her thumb today." She turned down the volume on the TV. Wade threw her a dirty look, but she didn't notice.

"No kidding?" Daddy folded up the newspaper. "She found her thumb all by herself?"

"One of the orderlies has been trying to teach her for quite some time in the hope she wouldn't cry so much."

Mom eased down on the couch next to Daddy and snuggled under his shoulder. "Apparently, every time he passed Krista's crib, he would stick her thumb into her mouth to help her stop crying. Today, I left the room, and Krista started to cry. But she stopped almost immediately. When I went back in to check on her, she was sucking her thumb and trying to sleep."

Mom wore the same proud expression on her face

like she does when I bring home all As on my report card or when Paul hits a double in baseball.

"I can't believe you *want* her to suck her thumb." Wade held up his own thumb. "You used to yell at me and tell me it was a bad habit."

She pulled him onto the couch beside her but kept talking to Daddy. "You know, it was such a relief not to have to hold her all day or listen to her scream. For the first time, I could put her down, and we could both get a little peace."

I viciously flipped the next page of *Strawberry Girl,* my temper not at all as gentle as my latest heroine's. Mom had told me all I needed to know. Krista *had* been unhappy every single minute at the hospital. She needed to come home. Even Strawberry Girl would have agreed with me there.

Chapter 12:
Hospital Visit

Ladies in white clothes
Sting my feet and sting my head.
Ow! I want Mah-mi.

After *four* days of no school because of an ice storm, there was finally something to do. Daddy let me go with him to visit Krista in the hospital. He said it'd be a surprise for Mom. As long as I was right beside him, the big bosses would let me visit. After all, I had started into my thirteenth year, but it was another eight months until my birthday. I could hardly wait to get to Krista.

Until we got to the hospital.

It was horrible. Huge. Ugly. *Gray.* As bad as I remembered from my tonsil operation days. Daddy set a brisk pace on stone-gray linoleum floors as we passed between dingy off-white walls. Everyone looked grim. The halls were mostly silent, broken only by an occasional voice paging a doctor over the loudspeakers. Silent people walked right past each other in rubber-soled shoes without making eye contact with anyone, like zombies in the movies I'd heard about.

I could taste the medicine and sickness every time I took a breath. The smell of pine cleaner mixed with ammonia was so strong they must have mopped the floors every hour. Add the scent of rubbing alcohol floating through the air, and all I could think of was getting shots.

Daddy slowed his steps. "Are you okay, Debbie?"

"Yeah…" I could hear the weakness in my voice.

"Shall I take you back to the car? You don't have to do this if you don't want to."

"No. I want to keep going."

He reached for my hand, covering it in warmth, so different from the cold indifference of this place. The strength in his grip offered protection.

"Daddy?"

"Mmm?"

"Nobody smiles here, not even the nurses. Don't they care?"

"Sure, they do. But it's a serious place. People come here with serious problems."

Maybe all those zombie-looking people didn't look at each other because they were afraid to find out about someone else's troubles. They already had enough of their own.

As we made our way through endless, dreary passages, I wanted to run away, flee outdoors, inhale fresh air, and bedazzle myself with the colors of spring. For the first time, I worried Krista *really* might die. Who could get better in a place like this?

I felt sick to my stomach.

We passed by the ladies' room. Maybe I could go

in there and splash cold water on my face to feel better. I dropped Daddy's hand.

"I'll be right back."

When I pushed the door open, a black and *gray* pattern of linoleum greeted me. I backed out in a hurry.

"You don't need the restroom after all?" Daddy cocked his head to the side, a puzzled expression on his face. How could I explain the color of the floors made me feel worse? He didn't need a crazy daughter on top of all his other troubles.

At last, we reached the entrance to Krista's hallway. Heavy, steel double doors, gray of course, prevented us from traveling farther. If I stood on tiptoe, I could see through small plates of glass in the center of the door. Wire mesh was set in the middle of the glass. The message was clear. *Stay out.* Daddy and I would have to communicate with Mom and Krista through the little windows.

Mom must have been waiting for him because she immediately stepped from one of the rooms and walked toward us with Krista in her arms. She wore a green surgical gown. A doctor's mask stretched over her nose and mouth and tied behind her head. Her eyes widened in surprise when she saw me peep through the window, and she threw a sharp, questioning glance toward Daddy.

He reassured her with a smile and motioned for her to hold the baby up to the window. Mom's eyes relaxed a little, then crinkled at the corners as she smiled beneath the mask and lifted Krista closer.

Krista was much tinier than I remembered. So pale. Baby dolls had rosier cheeks. I tapped at the window, but she didn't seem to notice. I waved. Her head turned slightly, but there was no toothless grin of welcome. *Had she forgotten me?*

Her eyes were dull, rimmed in red, and her mouth continually quivered, although she didn't cry. No wonder Mom came home sad and exhausted every night.

My face must have shown the shock I was feeling because Mom lowered her mask and smiled apologetically as though I blamed her for the sorry condition of my sister. If I started to cry, I knew Mom would cry, too, so I forced a smile.

With inches of steel door between us, no one could say anything without shouting. Hospitals frowned on loud voices. I mouthed, "I love you," and motioned for Mom to give Krista a kiss for me, which she did. Then I left. Fast.

As gloomy as the rest of the visitors, Daddy and I made our way back to the entrance. Once outside, sunshine warmed the freezing fog inside of me. Salt air combined with exhaust from the traffic on the nearby highway smelled a whole lot better than what lurked *inside* the hospital. When we reached the parking lot bordered by small evergreen bushes still glazed with ice crystals, I broke down in sobs.

"How can Mom stand it? Krista looks so weak and sick and helpless. And she's *sad.*"

He put his arms around me and hugged me so tightly I could barely breathe. "Mom knows Krista needs her right now. Mothers can stand anything if they have to. So she's strong enough to stay in this unhappy place with her sick baby, and she's strong enough to come home and give love and attention to her other children, too."

He cupped my face in his hands. "Are you sorry you came? Should I have made you stay home?"

"No." I wiped tears off my nose. "I'd rather know bad things than not know anything at all." I sniffed. "Now I understand better what Krista is going through. And what Mom is going through. I'm glad I know… even if it makes me cry."

"That's my girl." He gave me another squeeze. "I didn't think it was a mistake to bring you." He leaned against the side of the car. "I'd like to go back and visit with Mom a little while longer. Do you want to go back with me?"

"Can I stay here and read my book? I don't want to go back inside." I curled my fingers around the car door's handle, ready to hang on if Daddy tried to pry me off. "I think I would die if I had to stay in this place. Kids need to see sunshiny yellows and grassy greens and bright reds. Not an awful gray."

"Are you sure you want to stay here all by yourself?"

"Yes. And I'm sure I don't want to go back in that hospital. Ever."

"Even if they paint the walls using every color in the rainbow?" He tweaked my nose like I was still a little kid.

"Well, maybe then."

"I'll try to find a suggestion box and tell them to make the place brighter."

He unlocked the car, and I dove inside.

"The sun should keep you warm enough in there, but I won't stay long. Keep the doors locked." He watched me push the lock button down before he strode away.

Ever since that eye-opening visit, I asked detailed questions about Krista's progress. Did she cry much today? Did she need pain medicine? Did she get a shot? What did the doctor say? Did she eat enough? Did she smile?

I wanted to live the minutes with her.

Mom answered all my questions, and I gradually began to understand Krista's daily routine.

Every morning, they weighed her. She had dropped to six pounds, less than when she was born, but she was slowly starting to regain ounces.

Right after the operation, they took her temperature every hour. But a week later they only did that three times a day. At first, she had to take antibiotics through an IV tube attached to her head. They stuck a needle into a vein in her scalp, and medicine went right into her bloodstream. After a while, they took out the IV and poured her medicine into a dropper. Then they would put drops of medicine on her tongue, which Mom said was kind of tricky. Just like she did with the nipple on her milk bottle, Krista would push the dropper out of her mouth.

Then it was time for dressings to be changed. They took off old bandages, put special soap on her stitches, and put clean bandages on the incision that stretched from her chest around to her back at least once a day.

Bath time and feeding times were part of the routine, too. She was supposed to have a nap time, but Krista was never on schedule. She didn't sleep much. She probably hurt all over even with pain medication, and the dreary gray hospital wouldn't help *anybody* rest.

If she fell asleep at bath time, Mom skipped the bath and let her nap. The nurses said Krista slept at night, but I didn't believe them.

Krista was due to come home on Monday, January thirty-first, exactly three weeks after her operation. Her weight had climbed to seven pounds—still newborn size—but the incision had healed, and the doctors said she could continue to recuperate at home. Good. She'd get stronger a lot faster in her comfy house with family around who would *smile* at her.

I got home from school on Friday, only three more days to wait. The aroma of fresh, hot coffee welcomed me, and I discovered Mom curled up in an easy chair reading a magazine. Had she left Krista all alone? Was that a good thing or a bad thing?

"How come you're not at the hospital?" I tossed my coat over a chair.

"I decided to come home early. How was your day?"

"Great! We're planning a puppet show, and Miss Kay is going to let me write one of the scripts. If we're really good, she'll have us perform them for the kindergarteners."

Even though I felt sorry for Krista, I was feeling glad—and guilty—to have Mom to myself for once.

She smiled. "How exciting."

"Yeah. We're in groups of six, one writer and five actors, so the story needs five characters. Since I'm writing, I won't have a puppet." I started toward my room. "I'm going to work on it right away."

"Have fun." Mom turned a page in her magazine.

She seemed so relaxed.

"Did Krista have a good day? Is that why you're home now?"

"Yes, she had a good day." Mom smiled again. "By the way. I left a surprise in your room."

I trotted down the hall. "I bet I know what it is."

Three of my friends had gotten their first pair of stockings at Christmas. I'd been begging for a pair all month, but with Krista at the hospital, Mom was probably too busy to buy any.

I entered my room. No small package on my blue bedspread or doily-covered dresser. As I stood by the door, perplexed, a small rustling sound from the crib caught my attention. Or had I imagined it? I peeked over the headboard.

Snuggled under a soft yellow blanket, Krista slept peacefully in her own bed. Tears pricked my eyes and sniffles tickled my nose as I rested my head against the crib railing. I breathed in the wonderful scent of baby powder and whatever else made babies smell so good. Mom tiptoed into the room and kissed my cheek. She handed me a Kleenex then tiptoed out.

For the rest of the afternoon, I sat on the bed composing my puppet play. The slight *scritch, scritch* of pencil on paper was the only sound besides Krista's baby snuffles when she shifted positions. Paul and Wade stepped in several times just to stare at her.

Every few minutes I rested my pencil and glanced over at Krista. How could I have gotten used to an empty crib? This was life the way it was meant to be. My baby sister home to stay. Home with a mended heart.

Chapter13:
The Pack Meeting

Just Mah-mi and me
All day long 'til kids appear
To hold me and play.

For this whole school year, Mickey Hinkley had popped up almost everywhere I went. The bus, recess, my house. Nancy said I should tell him to get lost, but I felt sorry for him. He was almost fourteen and still in sixth grade. While his blond hair and freckles were cute, his nose was too large, his chin too small, and he always tripped over everything. I didn't have the heart to tell him to leave me alone, so we talked a little every day.

Well, *he* talked, always boasting about how great he was at baseball, or his fantastic fishing trips with his uncle. I didn't believe a word. He probably got tangled in his own big feet racing for a long fly ball. And an eight-foot shark? Whoppers like that showed why they're called, "fish stories.".

I asked Mom if there was any way to stop him from talking to me without hurting his feelings. She told me to "be nice."

So I tried not to cringe when Mickey slid next to me again on the bus. Nancy's class was late leaving the building, and we weren't allowed to save seats.

He flipped long bangs off his face. "Hey. No ball practice tonight. I'll come over after dinner."

A great time to use my number one excuse to say no—taking care of Krista. In the last two months since getting home from the hospital, she'd gained four pounds! Her sparkling smile had returned the first week home, and she'd gotten strong enough to roll from her back to her tummy. She was so healthy that Mom was willing to let me take care of Krista for a short amounts of time.

"You can't come over tonight. Everybody will be at the Cub Scout meeting, and I have to babysit my sister."

Pack meetings were the most boring things on earth except for when everybody shouted, "Wow! Wow! Pow!" And not even all that noise coming from fifty little boys was worth the rest of the two hours of flags and marching and boring speeches from the pack leader giving out badges. I had begged to be allowed to stay home. I even promised to wash *and* dry the dishes.

Mickey's response to my "no" almost changed my mind.

"Great." He looked at me like an evil gunslinger leering at Miss Kitty, the saloon girl in *Gunsmoke*. "Then your brothers won't be around to bug us."

Fifty screaming cub scouts were beginning to look more entertaining.

"Don't come over." I sighed as if I had the worst, most unreasonable parents. My next line of defense. "I can't have friends over when no one else is home."

Mickey shrugged, then smiled. "Okay. I get it."

When the bus stopped at his corner, he winked at me before he ambled down the aisle and made his exit.

Not fifteen minutes after everybody left the house, I heard a knock on the door. Guess who?

Chilly March air with a hint of woodsmoke poured through the screen door, and I pulled my sweater close around me. "What do you want?"

Rude, but Mickey *knew* not to come over.

"Just dropped by to say *hi*." He leaned one arm on the doorframe and spoke in a slow, lazy voice.

"Okay. Hi. Now you can go back home."

"Kind of touchy, aren't you? What's the matter?" He played with the door handle and discovered it was locked.

"You're not supposed to be here."

"You afraid of me?" He grinned.

"Of course not." Although I sure wasn't feeling sorry for him anymore.

"Then why don't you let me in?"

"No."

"You're afraid."

"Am not."

"If you're not, open the door."

Against house rules I unlocked the door and held it open. There. I'd proved I wasn't afraid.

Mickey walked up real close to me. *What had he eaten for dinner?* His breath smelled like limburger cheese. I hated the smell of *any* cheese.

"Nice kitchen, but why don't we sit in the living room?" He nudged me toward the couch.

Now he was scaring me.

I needed some distance between us to give me time to figure out how to get rid of him. "I think I hear Krista. I'll be back in a minute."

I ran to the bedroom, where the baby was sound asleep, and I hovered over the crib trying to come up with a solution. If I stayed away for more than a minute, Mickey would probably follow me down the hall.

"Just tell him the truth," I coached myself. "Tell him you don't like to deliberately disobey your parents." As I pushed away from the crib and turned to walk toward the door, another body slammed into mine, and strong arms tightened around me. Mickey's voice, creepy in the dark room, whispered, "Now, I've got you."

I sensed his face searching for mine. Was he going to force me to *kiss* him? This was why my parents told me not to let anyone in the house when they weren't home.

Like the Tasmanian Devil in a Bugs Bunny cartoon, I screamed and kicked and punched. "Let me go! Let me go! Let me go!"

My foot connected solidly with Mickey's shinbone. He let go and backed away. "What's the matter with you?"

In the lighted hallway, he stood on one leg and rubbed his shin, acting as if he were the injured party. Come to think of it, he *was* injured. Paul and Wade would've been proud of my defense moves.

"Get out! Get out of my house. And don't come back." I chased him down the hall, through the kitchen, and out the door. I didn't stop yelling until he hobbled past the end of the driveway.

My fingers shook so badly I could barely relock the door. Then I returned to the bedroom to check on Krista. That baby could sleep. With all the screaming, my brothers would have come running to my rescue from the back yard, but Krista, a few feet away, never woke up. She hadn't even rolled to her other side.

When the family came home, the house was as peaceful as when they left.

"Everything go smoothly?" Mom asked.

I looked up from my book. "Krista's been asleep all night." At least that part was true.

Chapter 14:
What Do Doctors Know?

Mouths fascinate me.
They make different shapes to name
Lots of different things.

Mom walked into the house and put Krista in her playpen in the living room. Then she sat at the kitchen table, laid her head on her arms, and cried. Really cried, like I used to do when I'd fallen off my bike and blood was running down my leg.

What had happened? Krista was just supposed have a regular check-up this afternoon. I'd been waiting to hear if she gained another two pounds. Ever since the operation three months ago, she'd never been sick, and her first tooth came in last week.

Mom had never sobbed like this, not even when Krista had her surgery.

I laid down my crossword puzzle book and stood next to her. *What should I do?*

"Mom?" My fingers brushed the stiff cotton sleeve of her jacket.

Her shoulders stopped shaking, but she didn't answer.

"Is something wrong with Krista?"

She sat up, grabbed a paper napkin from the holder, and wiped her eyes. She dabbed at her nose.

"No. Yes." She stared at the table. "I don't know."

I didn't see anything wrong with Krista. Her grin automatically brought out a grin from the rest of us. She gurgled baby noises, drank her milk, slept all night, and pooped through the day. Normal baby stuff.

Mom took a deep, shaky breath. "Dr. Winkler says Krista is mentally retarded."

The tapping of wood against wood as Krista played with blocks filled the silence following that statement. *Mentally retarded?* I pictured the clever sparkle in Krista's eyes. The doctor was wrong.

Mom sniffed and snatched up another paper napkin. "He says she should be preparing to crawl, but she's only just learned to sit up without wobbling. He says she should be making some kind of baby talk, but that isn't happening."

"Maybe, but she gets this sly expression on her face when she sits in her highchair and throws Cheerios on the floor. Would a retarded baby *know* her mother didn't like that?"

She ignored my efforts at humor. "He says she'll never be able to go to a regular school, never learn to read or write, and we'll be lucky if she ever gets potty-trained."

I wanted to punch Dr. Winkler in the nose. What a quack.

After a final dab to her swollen eyes, she rose from her chair and walked carefully to the opposite end of the kitchen, chin up, back straight. She reminded me of the girls from long ago who attended finishing school. *Ladies* used to practice *excellent posture* by balancing books on top of their heads while crossing a room.

Mom continued her careful stride to the living room after she dropped the crumpled napkins into the trash can. I followed. She picked up the baby, who laughed and wrapped her skinny arms around Mom's neck. When Krista noticed my attention, she leaned away from Mom and reached for me.

"Give Mommy a kiss." I made smoochy noises.

Immediately, she put her lips to Mom's cheek.

"See? She's smart. She might not make baby sounds, but she knows how to get her message across."

"Just because she can communicate doesn't mean she's smart." Mom shifted Krista to her hip.

"But she doesn't have the same eyes that Down Syndrome kids have."

"No, she doesn't have Downs, but German measles still could have damaged her brain." She pressed her cheek against Krista's. "Debbie, the doctors know their business, and look at the facts. Your sister doesn't babble normal baby sounds, doesn't try to get to her knees. She doesn't pay attention to very much going on around her. She's way behind other babies her age."

"I still don't think she's mentally retarded." I refused to back down. "I *prayed* she wouldn't be."

"Sometimes God doesn't answer prayers the way we want Him to."

"I know, but I'm sure God answered this one. When you told me what types of things could be wrong with the baby, I prayed she wouldn't be mentally retarded, that if something had to be wrong, she'd be blind or deaf instead, but—"

"Debbie, how *could* you?" She squeezed Krista so hard, the baby frowned and tried to struggle out of her grasp.

"—not both." I finished on a lame note.

"How could you pray for her to be blind or deaf?"

"I didn't. I mean, that wasn't my first choice."

Why was she so mad?

My fingers curled into fists. "First, I wanted everything to be okay, but if God said no, then I wanted her to still be able to read books. Deaf people can read books. Blind people can read braille books. But I don't think mentally retarded kids can learn how to read big books." Mom seemed to be listening.

"And if I had a choice between blind or deaf, then I wanted her to be able to see beautiful things like trees and the ocean rather than to hear."

"Stop it. Stop talking like that."

She *wasn't* listening.

"But Mom, she never looks around when we call her name. She doesn't even notice when jets break the sound barrier and the whole sky booms."

"I don't want to hear any more." She turned away and started to march at double-pace toward the bedrooms.

I followed, wanting to finish my point. "I think Krista doesn't hear our voices or the jets or the booms. Or thunder, or when Wade drops—"

"Debbie!" She bellowed my name. "I said *stop it*." And she ran into my bedroom still clutching Krista to her chest.

I didn't get it. The whole time Mom was pregnant she knew there would almost certainly be problems. So I prayed for the least of the problems if they had to happen at all. And sure enough, there were problems. The heart surgery, the cataract on her eye. But Krista could see, and she obviously understood lots of stuff. She tried to follow us all over the house by sliding on her tummy, and she tried to play with Wade's toys the same way he did. God had answered my prayer.

Mothers must look at things differently. Even when they've been warned what to expect, all they want is for their baby to be perfectly fine.

But Krista wasn't perfectly fine. Doctors had fixed her heart, and they might be able to fix her eye. If she were deaf, could they fix her ears?

But if they were right and I was wrong, they couldn't fix her brain.

Chapter 15:
Bullies and Babies

I love Oh-we-ohs.
My teeth bite them, but watch out.
They bite my thumb, too.

The only good thing about that doctor visit back in April was that Krista wasn't scheduled to go back until she was a year old. After Mom yelled at me to stop talking about Krista being deaf, neither of us mentioned it again, but I kept renewing a book from the library about sign language.

So far, she could wave her fist for *yes* and put her fingertips together for *more*. She couldn't make her fingers work right for *no*. I was learning signs for animals and people in the family, too. Krista could do them, sort of--baby talk with her hands. I figured if hearing babies can't speak words correctly for a couple of years, it would probably take Krista that long to make the signs just right.

Meanwhile, I didn't have to think about doctors and their stupid opinions until September. Something else to stuff in the closet of my mind.

By June, Krista, at nine months old, could get herself into almost as much trouble as any other baby who had figured out how to move. She still didn't crawl, but she could scoot around on her bottom or slide on her stomach, using her arms to pull her along from either position.

On Saturday morning when I ambled into the kitchen for my daily dose of orange juice, the entire room smelled like Hershey, Pennsylvania, the chocolate capital of America. Krista sat on the floor, coated in chocolate crumbs. Her cheeks were so stuffed with cookies she looked like a chipmunk. She tried to smile, which allowed bits of cookie to spill from her lips and stick to her chin. Her chocolate brown eyes matched the cookie crumbles on her face. One sticky hand gently massaged specks of Oreo into her scalp while the other dug into the bag for the next cookie.

Maybe I should've pointed to her and signed *bad*, but I didn't have the heart. She was having such a good time. Instead, I helped myself to an intact cookie sitting by its lonesome in the cupboard. Next, I yelled, "Mom! Come quick!"

Wade and Paul ran into the kitchen, took in the scene, and cracked up. Mom and Daddy arrived as we hopped all over the room, our bare feet landing on more crumbs with every step. My stomach hurt from laughing too hard.

"Oh, Krista!" Mom stared at the mess all over her baby. "Look at you. *Look* at you!" The half empty bag crackled as she snatched it from Krista's hands.

Why hadn't I thought to do that?

"Wasn't anyone watching her?" Daddy glared at

the mess all over the kitchen. "Who got her out of bed?"

At that point Wade should've sobered up, but he didn't. "Me," he gasped. "I didn't know she could get into anything."

Krista might have been way behind in the crawling department, but nothing was wrong with her fingers. They were totally capable of pulling open cupboard doors. By the looks of her, those fingers had no problem opening a new bag of cookies either.

Another glance at his polka-dotted sister and Wade redoubled his laughter, unaware of Daddy's red face. Which wasn't smiling.

"What a way to start a Saturday." He turned with a jerk at Mom's smothered giggle. "You think this is funny, too?"

"I can't help it. She looks like Tar Baby in the Brer Rabbit stories." She struggled to look stern but failed. Her forehead wrinkled and her lips tightened like she was ready to cry, but then she let go with a guffaw as loud as us kids.

"Tar Baby?" Daddy's favorite Uncle Remus story. He looked from Krista to Mom, and back to Krista. His face reddened even more. He broke into a grin. The redder he got, the wider the grin, until he laughed so hard tears rolled down his cheeks and he had to sit down. On the chocolate-covered chair.

June also meant corn on the cob. July would be the peak time for Long Island corn sweetness, but Mom always started buying it as soon as the weather could be expected to stay warm.

For our first Corn on the Cob Night of the year, Mom made sure we ate outside on our back patio. Warm sun, brisk ocean breeze, no mosquitoes. Perfect. Krista was stripped down to nothing but the rubber pants covering her diaper. Time to introduce her to the delights of butter dripping from every kernel.

Would heaven be like this? Perfect temperature. Every morsel of perfect food delighting the tongue. Perfectly happy people. My Sunday school teacher told me that God bans fear and sadness from heaven. As I took my first bite and the kernels popped salt and sweet inside my mouth, the fear-filled, gray days at the hospital almost disappeared from memory. *Almost* heaven.

"Look, Krista." Paul handed her half an ear of corn while holding a whole one of his own.

Krista watched him bite into it, and then she copied him. Her four teeth only slid along the slippery kernels.

Wade waved his corn in her face. "Watch me." He bit deeply into the kernels and growled, shaking his head like a dog defending its bone.

Krista gave it another go. Holding the corn with both hands, she slammed her mouth against rows of greasy kernels. Nope. Still no luck.

We gave up on the corn-eating lesson and gave in to the bliss of sweet, salty, crunchy gold.

Even if Krista couldn't figure it out, we knew she liked the taste of butter. She persisted in gluing her mouth to the corn until she finally dug in with the ferocity of a tiger and ripped away three kernels.

"Yay, Krista!" All of us clapped with butter-greased hands.

She grinned and attacked it again. By the time Mom handed around ice cream sandwiches, stray kernels rested in Krista's hair and dotted her face. Plastered with butter and corn from forehead to toes, she reveled in her new role as entertainer. Wade and Paul laughed so hard they about fell off the picnic bench every time another golden circle rolled to rest on her tummy, and she giggled right back.

When she spied several leftovers on her high chair tray, mischief sparkled in her eyes. She picked up one kernel and tossed it at them. Of course, it only made it to the edge of her tray, but not bad for a little kid who supposedly wasn't capable of understanding funny games and teasing. *What do you think about that, Dr. Quack-quack?*

Paul took up her challenge. "So you want a war, huh?" He picked up her corn bomb hanging off the high chair tray and aimed for her chest. Bull's eye.

Krista's chin lowered to search for the landing zone, and she picked off a different piece of corn from her stomach to throw back.

Before Paul or Wade could send off another salvo, Mom stretched a hand toward the middle of the table in a stop motion. "No food fights. Very bad manners."

"But we're outside." Paul's hand was still poised to send a kernel flying forward.

"I don't want you teaching your little sister that it's okay to throw food. She sends enough to the floor as it is."

The boys looked to Daddy to back up their side of the argument. He stifled a grin and shook his head. "Listen to your mother."

Defeated in mid-battle, they asked to be excused.

Permission granted. Mom wadded up a bunch of paper towels and started the wipe-down on Krista before starting a new mess of ice cream.

But when it came to school, June wasn't much fun. That ice storm back in January cost us three extra days of school to make sure there were 183 days for the year. Everybody got cranky with summer vacation delayed. Kids. Teachers. Parents.

The fight started because Jimmy Pulizzi called another kid a "retard." The "retard" was a shy, chunky boy who didn't have any friends. The poor kid had tried to tuck himself into a back corner of the crowded bus and hope for invisibility, but Jimmy followed him.

As he swaggered toward the kid, I flew out of my seat to block his way. "Why don't you leave him alone?"

He grinned, amused.

I took another step toward him. It was like watching myself from a distance. Debbie, who always had her nose in a book, stood nose-to-nose with the number one bully on the bus.

No way was I going to back down. "It's cruel to call people names."

He sneered. "Like 'retard'?"

"Yeah. My sister really *is* retarded." Since the doctors kept insisting Krista was retarded, I'd use the word as a badge of honor.

The normal babble on the bus cut to silence as I tore into him. "Do you ever *think* before you open your big, fat mouth? Do you ever think you might be ripping someone's guts out? *You're* the 'retard' around here."

Daddy once told me eyes are the windows to the soul. If you stare into someone's eyes, you can see what they're feeling.

I bored my gaze into Jimmy's eyes, noticing flecks of green in brown irises. I wanted him to see my anger.

And I wanted to know when he was about to punch me. At least I'd made my stand for all the Kristas in this world even if it earned me a bloody nose. I hoped it wouldn't hurt too bad.

As our eyes locked, I saw his soul.

The mockery disappeared, and in its place … shame. And… pain. Some kind of hurt all his own.

A flicker of understanding flashed between us, and my anger winked out like a lit match in the wind.

"Sorry," he mumbled, and slouched back to his seat.

I could barely make it back to mine, I was trembling so badly.

What had I just done?

For the rest of the stops, if kids talked at all, they spoke in whispers. Nancy gazed at me, her lips barely curved in a thoughtful smile. When I caught one of Jimmy's friends staring at me, he immediately shifted his gaze to a buddy across the aisle. A couple of the younger kids dared to grin at me—the girl who defeated the bully without lifting a finger.

But did they get it? That calling people nasty names *hurts?* That *all* unkind words hurt?

When we got off the bus, Paul landed a light punch on my shoulder. "I've never seen anybody light into Jimmy like that and live."

"Yeah, you showed him good." Wade punched my

other shoulder.

They'd never made me one of the boys before. But I couldn't forget the pain in Jimmy's eyes. I'd won the showdown using cruel words as a weapon.

I was no different than Jimmy.

Chapter 16:
Francie and Nancy

Nan-nee always moves
Her mouth. "El-lo, Oo-ihd-duh."
Fwan-nee ignores me.

"Here they come! They've still got the Green Giant." Paul trumpeted the news as he dashed into the house through the front door.

Wade and I almost bowled Paul over as we stampeded out the door, but his good reflexes allowed him to U-turn in time to join the rush in the opposite direction.

The extra-long, metallic green station wagon rolled to a stop in our driveway, and the back doors opened as we reached for the handles. Francie and I hugged each other, laughing and crying all at the same time.

My brothers and Vinnie rolled around on the front lawn, a tangle of tanned arms and legs, pummeling backs and shoulders and chests. They looked like a litter of puppies fresh from a nap.

Mr. Capelli waved at me, then began pulling the tarp off the roof rack. Mrs. Capelli slid out of the passenger side of their car loaded down with a gigantic pocketbook and a paper bag that probably held trash.

I ran over, hugged her, and grabbed the bag. A mix of warm banana peels and peanut butter assaulted my nose. "I'll get rid of this for you."

She gave me another squeeze. "Thank you."

On the way in, I passed Mom. She carried Krista who wore a brand new red and yellow-flowered sundress. When I ran back out, Mrs. Capelli was holding the baby and making all those coo-coo-coo noises. Krista loved it. She grinned at the new face.

"Dorothy, she's adorable." Mrs. Capelli planted a kiss on Krista's forehead. "After those first letters, I was still expecting a sickly, pale, under-sized infant."

Mom's eyes sparkled. "She's been thriving since February. She's gained nine pounds in five months."

"Well, you can see how lively this baby is."

They exchanged a long look, and then like Francie and me, they hugged like they'd never let each other go.

I grabbed Francie's hand. "C'mon. I'll show you my room."

Each of us plopped down on a bed just like old times

"I can't believe you're finally here." If I could've hugged the whole world, I would've done it.

"I know. Five whole days." Francie gazed around the room, beaming a thousand-watt smile. "This is almost like your room back home. Same bedspreads, same curtains."

I ran my finger down one ridge of the blue chenille bedspread and noticed a small hole in the worn fabric. I loved this bedspread. I'd had it as long as I could remember, but someday, I hoped for a new lavender one.

Francie pointed at the crib. "That sure wasn't in your room last year. And where's your desk?"

"In the basement. We had to make room for the crib and the changing table."

"You're okay with that? You never had to share a room before."

"I love sharing a room with Krista. She's no bother at all."

"You mean, she sleeps all night?"

"She's been sleeping through the night since before she went to the hospital for heart surgery." I held my hand mirror in front of her face. "Why? Are you worried about your beauty sleep?"

But she stayed serious. "I just can't imagine sharing my room."

If Francie never wanted to share her room, it was a good thing she never got a sister. I took a good look at my old best friend. Although we were only twelve, she'd transformed into a slim, tall teenager. No more baby fat. Deep blue eyes shimmered from a face framed by long, darkening blond hair. She looked like Candace Bergen. Gorgeous. Not one freckle.

Francie interrupted my thoughts. "What are you staring at?"

I shook my head, knocking the cobwebs out of my brain. "At you." I leaned across the narrow space between the beds and wrapped my arms around her again. "I can't believe you're here."

"Wow! The sand stretches forever." Francie had

never seen the ocean in her life.

"The beach is the best thing about living here."

"What's the worst thing?" she asked, renewing our old game of "Best and Worst Thing of the Week."

"You not being here to share the beach with me."

She grinned, satisfied.

We spread our beach towels a few feet away from the parents and lay on our backs letting the sea breeze waft over us.

Waft. I loved that word. Wind plus soft. Waft. Perfect.

Francie sat up, slathered more suntan lotion on her stomach, and handed me the bottle. Two-piece suits were new for us. We didn't want sunburns where the sun had never been before.

She nodded toward the rough surf. "We're not going to swim in that, are we?"

"Not me." I watched the water roll in, three waves piled on top of each other. They all broke together in a thunderous crash but didn't flow far. A strong undertow pulled them right back, maybe all the way to Africa.

"Only the strongest swimmers go out in this." I pointed to the flag at the end of the boardwalk. "See that? Red and white. You swim at your own risk."

Should I confess I was terrified of the breakers? Getting slammed onto a bed of broken shells hurts. When I was six, Daddy promised he wouldn't let go of me, and we would be fine. But a rough wave crashed over us, and he couldn't hold on. I thought I would drown before the tide sent me tumbling onto shore.

I decided not to share that story with Francie. She was nervous enough.

"Is it always like this?" She squinted out to sea.

"Naw. Sometimes it's as calm as Green Lakes." That's where we used to take swimming lessons back in Syracuse. I tugged on her hand. "We can still let the waves wash up to us."

My idea of fun was walking along the water's edge and letting the farthest ripples of each wave greet my toes. Francie let me drag her to where the last foam from the waves bubbled on the hardpacked sand.

I inched us further in. The ocean had finally started to get warm, almost seventy degrees, much better than the deep, snow-fed lakes of Upstate New York. We stood ankle-deep and let the waves splash against our knees, then swirl and pull powerfully at our heels. Francie adjusted her balance every few seconds. If a wave came in pretty strong, she grabbed my shoulder, almost knocking *me* off balance.

"Remember Lisa Stowe?" Francie nipped her lower lip with her front teeth. She always did that when she was nervous.

"Sure. She was really tiny with straight dark hair and the bluest eyes I've ever seen."

"We've gotten to be pretty good friends since you left." Again with the teeth and lip.

A twinge of jealousy poked me, but I batted it away. If I had a new best friend in Nancy, why shouldn't Francie have a new best friend, too?

Oh, my gosh. *Nancy.* Francie and I had talked so much last night, I forgot all about introducing her to Nancy. We could've run across the street while it was still light outside, but we kept talking. We barely remembered to put forkfuls of food in our mouths during dinner. And we talked all night until Daddy rapped on the door and threatened us with no beach.

When we got back to the house later, I'd have to take her across the street.

Francie squealed, interrupting my thoughts. "How did my feet get buried in sand?" She did a little hop-dance to pull free and run away from the water.

I watched the latest wave recede. My feet felt cozy as more sand piled over my ankles. I understood being scared of powerful waves. But afraid of sand?

Day three of Francie's visit, and we finally had time to stroll across the street to find Nancy. After a storm last night, it felt like fall already. No beach or pool. We took Krista with us. Nancy never missed an opportunity to hold a baby.

Her mom answered the door. "Hi, Debbie. Is this your friend from Syracuse?"

"Yes, ma'am. This is Francie. Is Nancy home?"

Mrs. McKenzie looked over her shoulder, then turned back to us. "I'm afraid Nancy isn't feeling very well today. Some kind of summer cold. If she feels better tomorrow, I'll send her over. Okay?"

"Okay." Confused, I stared at her. Nancy never got sick. In the eleven months I'd known her, not even a sneeze. Come to think of it, Nancy hadn't been her normal, wild and crazy self since school let out.

Francie and I turned back toward my house.

"I guess we can take Krista for a walk in her stroller." Usually, Nancy and I read books side by side on a day too cool for swimming, but Francie didn't like to read all day. She'd rather play kickball.

"She won't get sick, will she?" Francie asked.

"Who won't get sick?"

"Krista."

"Why would she get sick taking a walk?"

Francie raised her eyebrows like she was the queen of England or something. "My mom said she was so sick last winter, your parents were afraid she would die."

As scary as that time was, my parents never once used the word *die*. Francie didn't know what she was talking about.

"She needed an operation, and the operation worked. She's fine."

Francie's eyebrows rose a little higher. "Oh." She could still get snippy.

I stuffed Krista in the stroller and took off at a brisk pace. When the wheels bumped against the uneven sidewalk at high speed, Krista and the stroller bounced.

More, she signed. Her giggles thawed the cool silence between me and Francie, and together, we steered the stroller toward as many sidewalk cracks as we could spy.

Nancy's mysterious illness lasted for another two days, so Francie and I went to the pool and played Sharks and Minnows with everybody else. On the last day of her visit, we got another afternoon on the beach. The ocean was a lot calmer this time. I actually got beyond the breakers. When Francie saw how I did it, she timed the waves, too. It was kind of like judging when to hop in when you jump rope. Once she joined me, we let the gentle swells carry us along the shore.

"This is so cool." She stuck out her tongue and touched it to the water, then looked at me in surprise. "I didn't know you could actually *taste* the salt in the ocean."

I laughed. "Of course, you can. Why do you think it's called *salt water*?"

She paddled around, then squeaked in alarm when a stalk of seaweed curled around her wrist. "Eww! Slimy."

I unwound it and tossed it back in the water. "You'll have to come here every summer that we're still here. It's the best place we ever moved to." I floated on my back and let my legs kick me farther out.

She breathed a sigh of contentment. "Yeah. And maybe next year, I can meet Nancy."

"Yeah, maybe."

She side-stroked my way, brave enough to swim farther from the beach. "You think she was jealous that I came to visit?"

"I don't know."

Nancy was always so sure of herself. I couldn't believe she'd be afraid of Francie.

"I think Lisa would be jealous if you came to visit me."

A complicated question came to mind. "If you and I were best friends here, and if Nancy was my old friend who came to visit me, would you be jealous?"

Francie's sunburned cheeks turned a deeper shade of pink. She gazed toward the horizon. "I think I would."

I felt better about that little stab of jealousy when she mentioned Lisa the other day. "Me, too."

I spun in circles as I treaded water. "Remember when we were Brownies?"

"Yeah."

"Remember the song, 'Make New Friends?'"

She began to sing, and I joined her. "Make new friends, but keep the old. One is silver and the other gold."

We giggled and looked around to see if anyone was listening, but no one was nearby.

"What made you think of that?" she asked. The way she grinned at me, I could tell she knew the answer.

"Lisa and Nancy are silver," I said. "And you're gold."

Chapter 17:
Summer Blues

Deh-bee and Nan-nee
Are sad. Did they lose something?
I would be sad, too.

Nancy showed up at our front door almost as soon as Francie's station wagon had turned the corner on its way back to Syracuse.

"Hey." She flashed me a big smile. "Did y'all have a good time this week?"

"Yeah. It was great seeing Francie again." I kept quiet about the fact that I'd see her in August at summer camp.

"Too bad she lives so far away."

"Yeah." What was she getting at?

"You wanna ride bikes or something?"

"Okay."

We rode all over base housing, never saying a word to each other. Weird. Nancy always had something to say Finally, she stopped at the playground. She ran to the monkey bars and climbed to the top. I followed her but stopped at the second highest bars, then sat down so I could rest my arms on the top bar. She swung her legs back and forth and kept her back to me.

I couldn't stand it anymore. I had to ask. "Were you really sick this week?"

The rhythm of her legs paused, then started again. "I've been kinda sick all summer."

My heart picked up its pace. Was Nancy sick, like with cancer or something? My grandpa died from cancer.

She glanced at me then slipped her body downward and hung from the top bar by her knees. "I'm not really *sick* sick. But when I think about things, I *feel* sick."

That didn't make me feel any better.

She spit it all out then, hanging upside down and tearing our world apart.

"We're moving. My dad's been transferred to Arizona. I didn't want to ruin the whole summer for you so I didn't say anything."

All the excitement of starting junior high together had just turned into a nightmare of walking solo into a strange school.

She took my silence for what it was. Fear and anger.

"Are you mad that I didn't tell you?" She looked up at me, trying not to cry.

Which brought me to my senses. I wasn't the only one hurting here. But I was the one left behind.

"No, I'm not mad. Not at you." I met her gaze. "I just can't believe it."

She sighed. "We knew it would happen sooner or

later."

"Yeah." Something else I'd stuffed in the closet of my mind. I'd gotten awfully good at that. "So why are you telling me now instead of waiting until the day you move?" *Did that sound mean?*

"Because we move next week."

I couldn't breathe. We only had a week left? And I had spent the last five days with Francie. No wonder Nancy had felt sick. My face must have expressed exactly what I felt because she did start to cry. I climbed to the top rung, then hung upside down so we were eye to eye.

"What day do you leave?"

"July fifteenth."

I had only four days to make up the lost time from last week.

"So what do you want to do for the next four days?" I asked.

"Cry."

"That would be a waste." Somebody had to be strong here. I always thought it would be Nancy. "Let's plan something special each day. You know our moms won't say no."

"I want to pretend everything is normal."

"Okay. So one day we'll go to the beach. And one day we'll go to the pool. And one day we'll read books in my room. What else?"

She wiped her nose with the hem of her shirt. "Let's do the book day on moving day. I can stay out of the way and not even think about the moving van at *my* house."

We swung back to sitting positions. She was thinking hard now. "And let's go through the woods all the way to the railroad tracks."

"Okay. We'll take pennies with us." Parents were forever warning their kids to stay off the tracks. The kids paid no attention. "And lunch."

Nancy finally smiled. She always liked a good plan.

Mom's voice intruded upon General Sherman's destruction of Atlanta, and I raised my eyes from *Gone with the Wind*. Her turquoise shorts and tanned legs jolted me out of a world of hoop skirts and pale complexions.

"Debbie, go outside. It's a beautiful day."

I huffed. "If I go outside, I'll only get more freckles."

If I had lived in the 1860s, the world would've scorned me for ugly. Scarlett O'Hara, the heroine in my book, scrubbed lemon juice on any freckle that dared to appear on her perfect face.

With hands on her hips, Mom's sandaled foot tapped a fast beat on the wood floor. "Don't be ridiculous. Your freckles are adorable."

Said the person who never got freckles. I rose from my favorite reading chair. One more defeat in the war of wills. Mom five million, Debbie zero. I shuffled toward the back door, book in hand, which she snatched as I passed by.

"I don't want you reading outside, for pity's sake. I want you *playing* outside. Moving, running, doing cartwheels."

Yeah, right. That was me. On my way to a gold

medal at the Olympics. If I looked her in the eye, she'd read my thoughts.

"And put some shoes on!"

My sneakers lay under Krista's crib along with her giraffe. I tossed the stuffed toy over the railing, yanked open my sock drawer, and slammed it shut. If she woke up, at least I'd have someone to keep me company. No such luck. I hadn't really expected the bang from the drawer to wake her. It never had before, but I'd hoped the giraffe thumping onto her mattress would disturb her.

Outside, no kids ran around in the common area that connected all our back yards. Little ones were napping. Bigger kids were probably at the base pool. Paul and Wade had headed for the woods right after lunch.

I didn't want to go with them. Nancy wouldn't be there, and I wanted to hang onto our last good time together. We had filled Wade's knapsack with junk food and sodas, spent all day on the sandy trails, laid pennies on the tracks, and returned to find them the size of quarters once the trains had passed by.

I'd already written her two letters. She'd written back once. I didn't expect many more once school started. That's the way things usually happened in the Air Force. People moved on. The next base, the next school, the next house, the next friend.

It was bad enough that I lost Francie last year, but at least we could still see each other once in a while. Unless my dad got transferred to Arizona, that wasn't going to happen with Nancy and me. And I'd be in college or all grown up before Krista and I had much in common. Bummer.

It didn't used to be so difficult to find a new friend. *Little* kids just played together. Their moms made sure they met at a park or went to each other's houses, but now… I was too old for my mom to call somebody else's mom and invite a kid over. I was too shy to push myself on someone new, unlike Nancy who had pushed herself on me.

Why did I always assume someone wouldn't want my company? I had welcomed Nancy's. With junior high, my problem would only get worse. Once a girl had a best friend, other girls weren't all that welcome. Like Rita and Candi. We used to be two pairs of best friends. Nancy and Debbie, Rita and Candi. Now, we were a lopsided trio. It didn't feel right.

Besides, those two were more boy crazy than ever. Their parents actually allowed them to go on dates to the movies last winter. In *sixth grade*. My run-in with Mickey back in March proved I wasn't ready for the kind of girl-boy stuff Rita and Candi always talked about.

So since Nancy left, I'd been sitting around the house listening to Beatles records by myself, reading Dana Girls mysteries by myself, even playing board games by myself. I'd always liked some alone time, but I didn't want weeks of me and nobody.

With no action in the back yard, I headed toward the sidewalk and ambled in the general direction of Rita's house. Listening to her swoon over Lee Majors from *The Big Valley* had to be better than hours of playing catch with a kickball bounced off the garage wall.

Rita's front door opened as I crossed her front yard. She and Candi barged out, arms around each other, laughing at some hilarious joke. As soon as they saw me, they stopped. No further forward motion, no more giggles. They stood side by side and exchanged a glance.

"Hi," I offered.

"We were just heading over to my house," Candi said. She walked toward the sidewalk, tugging Rita with her.

"All right." I fell into step behind them.

They stopped and traded off another glance.

Candi turned to face me. "Look, Debbie. *Rita* and I are going to my house."

I had just walked into one of my worst nightmares. My heart pounded so hard I could hear it. "So because Nancy's not around, the three of us can't hang out?"

I wanted the straight truth. No more pretending things were okay.

Candi wrinkled her nose as if she'd gotten a whiff of fresh dog poop. "I have no idea why Nancy wanted you for a friend. But until you lose a little weight and gain a little pizzazz, I really don't want to hang out with you."

Well, I got my straight answer. And Jimmy Pulizzi passed by us on the sidewalk just as she shot off her mouth. Those killer words probably made his day.

Candi waited for my reaction. She thought I would cry in front of a jerk? And I didn't mean Jimmy. At least, I was getting a little curvy. She was built like a toothpick.

I glanced at Rita, her eyes wide, like she couldn't believe Candi insulted me to my face. But she didn't defend me.

"I won't be bothering you again." I walked back

the way I came.

"Debbie?" Rita's voice.

I stopped without turning.

"Sorry."

"Me, too." I resumed my steps and never looked back.

Behind Rita's house lay a no-man's land of scrubby pine trees, long grasses, and clumps of bushes. It sloped into a shallow valley, and taller pines lined the opposite hill. A single hawk circled overhead in a pale blue sky. Did it feel as lonely as me? Did the other hawks decide he was worthless? If the other hawks were anything like Candi, he was better off without them.

I walked down the slope until I came to a patch of clover near the bottom. Sitting cross-legged, I picked at various stalks counting petals on the clover. None of them had four leaves. No good luck for me.

Jets rumbled in the distance, a regular rhythm as each one took off. My dad probably sat in the cockpit soaring over the ocean with his pilot buddies while I plucked weeds in this lonely, dry valley.

I searched for the hawk. There he was, still riding the air currents. Alone. I would remain solo, too, until a *real* friend came around to join me.

"Where'd your Siamese twin go?"

I started at the voice that came out of nowhere. Jimmy Pulizzi circled my spot and plopped down in the grass across from me. I didn't need another enemy right now. Had he followed me here to gloat? Had he dropped a spider in my hair when he sneaked up behind me?

I glared at him. "What do you want?"

He shrugged. "Just asked a simple question. Where's Nancy? You two are always together."

"Not anymore." I yanked on another stem of clover.

"You weren't fighting over me, were you?"

I slid a sideways glance at him, refusing to laugh at his joke. His grin disappeared. "Oh, man, she moved, didn't she?"

I nodded.

"Is her dad going to 'Nam?"

I stopped pulling clover petals. "Why would you think that? They're in Arizona."

"Oh."

Silence stretched between us like a dry rubber band. Something was about to snap apart. After plucking another three-leaf clover, I looked up at him. He stared at something past my shoulder. When I turned to look, nothing seemed out of the ordinary.

"We're moving, too."

Good. I'd never have to worry about Jimmy Pulizzi's taunts ever again.

"To Queens."

As in part of New York City? I didn't think there was an Air Force base there.

I twisted back to face him. "Queens?"

"Yeah, we're gonna live with my grandparents."

"Are your parents getting a divorce?" I knew a lot of kids who had to choose whether to live with their dad or their mom. I had already decided neither one of them would get me if they broke up. I'd go live with Grandma.

"No divorce. We'll just live there while my dad's in Vietnam."

Every bad thing I ever thought about Jimmy came back and slapped me in the face. *Nobody* deserved the fear that invaded when fathers go to war. "I'm sorry."

He ducked his head in kind of a "thank you" motion. "We'll be okay."

"Yeah."

"But it will stink to have to go to a city school just for the year and then change again when he gets back."

"Yeah." I wasn't into moving a lot anymore either, but we'd probably have to transfer at least one more time before my dad retired.

Silence rested between us again, this time more like two old farmers in their rocking chairs on the front porch. After a while, Jimmy stood. "I gotta get home. The moving van comes tomorrow, and I'm supposed to pack what I want in my suitcase tonight."

I stood, too. "I didn't realize you were leaving right away."

"Yeah." His sad, crooked smile reminded me of a tragic hero from a romance novel.

Jimmy Pulizzi a romantic hero? *Was I out of my mind?*

"When I saw you walking down here, I thought I'd say goodbye." He held out his hand, and I shook it.

"I'm glad you did." And I meant it.

He turned to leave, then swung back toward me with the old, sassy grin on his face. "I wanted to tell you something else, too."

Uh-oh.

"You're not fat, and Candi's ugly."

I smiled as he raced up the hill and out of my view, but now I wore a double cloak of melancholy—Jimmy's fears and my sadness over Nancy. Strange to think he might have ended up a decent friend. Instead, both of us were alone.

Chapter 18:
Summer Nursery School

Little children play
But I am not allowed to.
Juice! Open the door!

I returned to plucking clover petals.

Other than a week at camp with Francie, the rest of the summer stretched out endlessly like the landscape. No friends and nothing to do. I was a wimp who was still afraid of ocean waves bigger than ripples on a lake. And I was freckle-face ugly.

All I wanted was for school to start again. To begin junior high without Nancy would be terrifying, but at least I'd be busy reading books, learning history, and singing in choir. Once I was done with high school, I'd go to college, and when I was done with college, I'd teach school until I was so old they'd have to roll me out at the end of each day in my wheelchair. School…

School?

School!

I dropped the clover and scrambled to my feet. *I could teach school for the rest of the summer.* Nursery school. When I counted all the houses on both sides of my street and around the block, there had to be at least a dozen little kids between the ages of two and four. I could make some money. I'd have a real job. The rest of summer would fly by.

As I walked faster and faster down the sidewalk, ideas raced into my brain, tripping over each other as they called for my attention. Music time, gym time, story time, snack time, lesson time. I could do this!

I grabbed pencil and paper from the kitchen counter on the way to my room. Sitting on the floor between the twin beds, my back against one box spring and my feet pressed against the other, I madly scribbled my list.

Mom passed my door and did a double take.

"What are you doing back inside?" she hissed in a stage whisper. "And get out of this room. Krista is taking a nap."

I forgot. Pushing to my feet, I scurried out of the room on tiptoe. Mom placed a hand on my shoulder and propelled me down the hall and toward the back door.

"Outside, Debbie."

"No, wait." I dragged my heels. "Wait." I waved the notebook and pencil like a Navy sailor signaling with flags. "What would you say if I promised to be outside every morning for two hours?"

She released her grip on my shoulder. "What do you mean?"

"I mean I've got this really great idea." I talked fast so she couldn't interrupt. "I'm gonna teach a nursery school. I'll take the little neighbor kids for two hours every day, and we'll sing and play games and drink Kool-Aid and eat cookies and do little art projects and have recess, and I'll read a picture book to them, and their moms will be glad to have them out of their hair for a little while, and they'll pay me." I took a deep breath. "So what do you think? Will you let me do it?"

Silence. Was it a stupid idea? It couldn't be. I was born to be a teacher. But did I forget something important?

The faraway screech of a sea gull sounded through the open window. I stared into Mom's eyes trying to figure out what she was thinking, but I couldn't read her expression. She nibbled on a thumb nail.

Finally, she said, "I think you'll need my help."

That meant yes!

"Oh, you won't have to help. There's fifteen kids that I counted up, and they probably won't all come every day. I can handle them by myself."

She shook her head. "Even real teachers, if they have fifteen students, also have other staff nearby, just in case. What if one of the children scrapes his knee? You'll have to take care of it or walk him home, and then who's going to watch the other fourteen?"

My happy balloon deflated.

Mom continued talking her thoughts. "It doesn't have to be me as the teacher aide. One of your friends could help out. But the moms will want to be sure that I'm home at all times."

Of course, a mom wouldn't trust a twelve-year-old to take care of her kid along with a dozen others. As for friend-helpers, I'd lost two possibles in the last hour. Rita and Candi wouldn't have worked out anyway. Rita would've wanted to sketch the latest fashions for preschoolers. Forget about playing Ring Around the Rosy. And Candi *hated* standing in the same room with little kids. Anyone under the age of seven was a mindless munchkin in her book.

Nancy would have been *glad* to be my teacher's aide.

"I don't think I have any friends who would help me."

Mom squeezed my shoulder in sympathy. "You miss Nancy, don't you?"

I nodded. If I tried to speak, my voice would crack.

"Your assistant doesn't have to be a friend from your class. Just someone old enough to be helpful with younger children. Like Laurie, maybe.

Laurie Gaston lived next door. She was ten, Paul's age. And she loved helping out with Krista, who at the moment crawled toward us and wrapped her arms around Mom's leg.

Mom opened the back door. "Let's sit at the picnic table and work out some details."

Summer wasn't looking so endless anymore. I was actually going to be a teacher. A good one.

"Can Krista be one of my students?"

"She's much too little," Mom replied. "Besides, you want all your students to be potty-trained. Right?"

Ewwww. One more thing I hadn't thought of.

Eight wiggle-worms dressed in a rainbow of colors sat in a circle in my back yard. Although the morning dew had evaporated, its fresh scent still hung in the air.

Three-year-old Terrence, in a red and blue-striped

shirt, spun on his bottom creating mashed circles in the grass. His gray shorts would have a noticeably green stain on the back side as soon as he stood up. No worries. His mom called him her little dust ball.

Angela, in her lemon-yellow sundress with matching shorts, sat cross-legged, her little sister next to her in pink.

"Now, Sherri." The tip of Angela's nose made contact with the toddler's forehead. "We gotta do exactly what Miss Debbie tells us, you hear? You can't go running around doing whatever you feel like."

Sherri stared at me from across the circle, her pale, round, china-doll eyes opened even wider. She popped her thumb in her mouth. Did Angela want to terrify her little sister?

I'd learned from helping out at Sunday School, there's always one child who tries to take the teacher's place. In this class, Angela was auditioning for the role. She was the tallest kid in the group and probably the oldest.

Of the eight who arrived for our first day of summer nursery school, I knew six of them well from the commons area behind our houses. But two little brothers from farther down the block and across the street had joined us. Identical twins. Their mom had dressed them so Joey was in green and Jimmy in tan. Jimmy also wore cowboy boots, all of which made it easy to tell them apart for today, but I planned to check every detail of their faces to figure out any differences. Freckle patterns? Chickenpox scars? Something.

I took a deep breath, ready to welcome the group and start a name game, when Angela stepped onstage as Teacher.

"Are any more kids coming, Miss Debbie?" She eyed the human spinning top. "Terrence, sit still. You're making me dizzy."

His circles slowed to a halt, and he joined the group of expectant faces directed my way. I caught Laurie's glance, who grinned, rolling her eyes toward Angela.

I dropped to the grass between Terrence and Joey. "I am so glad you guys came. Miss Laurie and I planned lots of fun things to do."

"Do we get snacks?" This from Kevin, who wore his toast and jam breakfast on his T-shirt.

"Yes, we get snacks, and we play games, and we sing songs."

"When is the snack?" Kevin again.

"Snacks always taste best when we're hot and thirsty. We've got some things to do first. And we're going to start with a name game." I motioned for Laurie to sit down, too. "Watch how Miss Laurie and I do it and think about what you want to say when it's your turn."

Laurie and I started a simple rhythm, two smacks on our knees, two claps on our hands. Smack-smack-clap-clap. "I am Deb-bie." Smack-smack-clap-clap. "I am tweh-ehlve." Smack-smack-clap-clap. "I like to read books."

Smack-smack-clap-clap. "I am Laur-ie." Smack-smack-clap-clap. "I am teh-en." Smack-smack-clap-clap. "I like ba-bies."

We stopped the rhythm. "See? How many of you know your names? Raise your hands."

A chorus of giggles and a show of eight hands, even silent little Sherri's.

Laurie asked, "Do you know how old you are?"

"Three."

"Four."

"Four and a half."

All the older kids had spoken, but Sherri's eyes rounded again, and my two other little girls didn't smile either.

I pointed at each one around the circle. "Terrence, Joey, and Jimmy are three. Kevin is four. Angela is four and a half, right?"

They nodded vigorously.

"And I happen to know …" I gazed around the circle with a smile. "Robin had a birthday last week. How many candles were on your cake?"

Robin's eyes sparkled. "Thwee."

"And Tammy is two. Her mom told me."

Tammy smiled in relief. She had a number.

"And Sherri is two," Angela announced.

"Right," I said. "So we're going to go from oldest to youngest, and we will all help the younger ones." I raised my eyebrows. "Now. I want you to think of something you like. What did I like in the name game?"

"To read books," Terrence answered.

"Right. And what did Laurie like?"

"Babies," said Robin.

"So here we go."

It took a while for everyone to get that smack-smack-clap-clap rhythm, but they seemed eager to try. We let the twos smack and clap whenever it moved them. Terrence liked football, the twins liked each other, Kevin liked snacks. Robin chose babies. It looked like Laurie had an admirer. To stick with the rhythm, Angela wisely kept her age to four but had trouble fitting "I like butterscotch pudding" into two claps. After much thought, and a dying away of smack-smack-clap-clap, Tammy liked Miss Debbie, and Sherri whispered something into her sister's ear. "Sherri likes Mommy," Angela announced.

The game took longer than expected, so I didn't have to worry about running out of things to do. We stood up for a few rounds of "Ring Around the Rosy" followed by "London Bridge is Falling Down." Of course, Terrence loved to fall down, big time, no matter which song we were singing. The kids laughed, and he ate up the applause. Little Miss Angela with her copper curls and neatly pressed sundress folded herself gently into a sitting position after every chorus.

At snack time, Mom carried out Hawaiian Punch and sandwich cookies on a tray but went right back inside leaving me in charge to serve it all. By this time, the kids were noisy and pretty comfortable with each other as they sat at the picnic table. When the food arrived, they quieted down. I gave each child two cookies, then lifted filled paper cups and handed them around.

Kevin accepted his with shining eyes. "I *love* Hawaiian Punch."

With a grin, I bopped the top of his head with one finger.

He tipped the cup toward his mouth and promptly dribbled punch onto his shirt. Good thing he was wearing red.

The twins dutifully thanked me as I gave them their cups. Terrence downed his drink in one long gulp. By the time he got to sixth grade, he'd probably add a loud belch for everyone's entertainment.

A strident, prissy voice shot out from the quiet munching on cookies and slurping of punch. "What's wrong with *her*?"

I turned toward Angela. "Who?"

"That little girl. What's wrong with her eyes?"

My eyes and everyone else's followed her pointing finger to Krista, who was crawling toward our table.

I never get huffy when people ask an honest question about Krista, but when someone puts the emphasis on "What's wrong with *her*," the question has a sneer attached.

Did Mom hear Angela through the open window? If the kid's mother wasn't paying me to teach the little snob, I'd be in her face like I'd been in Jimmy Pulizzi's back in June.

But teachers should control their tempers. I used my grown-up voice to answer Angela's dishonest question. "The muscles in her eye don't work right."

"Eyes have muscles?" Terrence raised his arms in a strong man pose, and the other kids laughed. Class clowns could be a blessing.

When Krista reached the bench, she struggled to her feet next to where Robin sat and smiled. Robin smiled back and pulled her onto the bench.

Krista tapped fingers to her lips. *Eat.* I gave her a cookie.

Sherri slid from her seat and walked around the table to stand by Krista. She reached up to caress my sister's face. "Baby," she said with all the tenderness of the Virgin Mary looking at her newborn Jesus. The first words she'd spoken all day.

Bless you, Sherri.

Chapter 19:
Summer Camp

Big animals sleep
Near a big, big house. I don't
Like big animals.

Even with the nursery school to keep me busy, August had dragged on and on, but in three hours, Francie and I would be together at camp. Not our old Camp Cayuga up by the Finger Lakes. Mom said she wasn't traveling that far. So the Capellis agreed to Hillside Camp in the Catskill Mountains. Daddy had wanted to stop at West Point since it was on the way, but I said let's do that on the way back next week. I would not wait one minute longer to see Francie.

Turning off the highway, our tires crunched on a gravel road for what seemed like forever before two lines of cabins appeared on the slope to our left, and a big barn-looking building on some flat space lay directly ahead of us. Behind the barn, ripples of mountains continued as far as I could see.

Families mobbed the tables that had been set up in front of the barn for registration. The ladies working at those tables didn't look happy. Maybe too many people asking too many questions all at the same time. If Francie was in one of the lines, I couldn't tell.

Daddy parked in an open spot between a sports car and another station wagon. Paul and Wade hopped out, ran around to the back, and opened the hatch.

"Not yet, guys." Daddy shut the hatch, keeping all of our gear in the car. "Let's get you signed in and find out which cabin is yours before we take anything out."

"Okay." The boys raced for the barn.

Mom strode toward the registration lines, so it was up to me to get Krista out of her car seat. Holding her on one hip, I ambled toward the barn. Krista gazed at all the action surrounding us. Kids ran in every direction. Old friends shouted greetings. A few younger kids cried as parents said good-bye. Grown-ups bustled across our path loaded down with sleeping bags and suitcases.

With just a few yards to go, I set Krista on her feet and held her hands over her head. We often practiced walking this way. The uneven dirt and gravel made it more difficult, but I figured she could handle the challenge. She probably would've tippy-toed her way toward Mom just fine, except for the dogs. Two big labs lay under the registration table. Krista wasn't keen on dogs. She stopped all forward motion.

"It's okay." I nudged my knee into her back, but she just looked at me, her fist opening and closing in baby sign for *no* and her eyes pleading for me to remove her from danger.

"They're nice doggies," I reassured her.

I picked her up and headed straight for the dogs. Paul and Wade were petting the golden one since the black one was asleep. When I bent down to pet the yellow dog and give Krista the opportunity to touch his silky ears, she climbed up my face and perched on top of my head, screeching. Crab-walking backwards as quickly as I could without knocking her to the ground, I must've looked pretty stupid. And the stony ground wasn't any too kind to my hands either.

So much for making a good first impression.

Mom looked down at me, annoyed.

Before she could say anything, I heard a welcome voice.

"Debbie!"

Francie snatched Krista from my head and shoulders, swung her onto a hip, and reached out her other hand to help me stand. As soon as I was on my feet, she squeezed the breath out of me.

She turned her attention back to Krista. "Do you remember me? I'm Francie. I saw you last month. You've already grown. What a big girl you are now."

Krista appeared stunned to be in this stranger's arms, but she looked down at the dogs and realized she was much farther away when Francie held her. She sparkled a smile back at her.

"She's adorable." Francie kissed Krista on both cheeks. "This is going to be so much fun. The girls in our cabin are really cool. You'll like them. We were some of the first people to show up, so I got to meet a lot of them already."

Mom relieved her of the baby burden. "Francie, it's good to see you."

"Hi, Mrs. Hansen. My parents already left for the

hotel. They said they'd meet up with you there."

"We're looking forward to dinner." Mom smiled at Francie and handed me a slip of paper. "Cabin Six, last one on the right."

"Cabin six?" Francie asked.

I consulted the paper. "That's what it says."

"Oh." Her voice had diminished. "I'm in Cabin Two."

We stared at each other. This couldn't be happening.

"Mom. When you sent in the application, you asked for us to be in the same cabin, didn't you?"

She frowned. "Yes, I did, but they were clear in saying they don't make guarantees."

"Can you see if I can switch with someone who hasn't gotten here yet?" I didn't wait all these weeks and not be able to live in the same cabin with Francie.

"Let me see what I can do."

Francie and I returned to the car while Daddy, Paul, and Wade lurched up the hill toward the second line of cabins loaded down with all their gear. I tossed Francie my sleeping bag and yanked out my suitcase and pillow. We sat on the bumper, swatting flies, and waited for Mom.

"I taught my own nursery school this summer."

"Yeah?"

"Yeah, four whole weeks, three days a week. I charged a dime per kid. Earned twelve bucks!"

"Twelve dollars?"

I nodded with the confidence of a savvy businesswoman. "A lot better than my seventy-five-cents-a-week allowance."

Mom turned away from the registration table, and

we ran to meet her. I could tell the news by the look on her face.

"I'm sorry, sweetie. Every bed has been assigned in Cabin Two. You're going to have to stay put."

I hunched into my shoulders. All our plans to do *everything* together for a whole week. Gone. Destroyed. Ashes in the wind.

"Can I move to Cabin Six?" Francie's eyes filled with tears.

"I think your parents would have to make that request." Mom wrapped an arm around Francie's shoulders. "The registration people made it pretty clear they don't change cabin assignments readily." Mom released her with a pat. "It won't be so terrible. You two will get to do activities together, just not sleep in the same room."

But that was the best part of camp.

When my cabin trooped into the dining hall, Francie waved from the far table of Cabin Two, making mad gestures that looked like swimming, then poking herself in the eye and pointing to me. After a tasteless dinner of chicken a la king and overcooked corn, the camp director announced how each cabin would do everything together except for the all-camp swims in the lake. I'd have to eat with Cabin Six, sit with them during chapel, and have craft class and swimming lessons with them. We'd have a softball tourney going every afternoon after lunch. Yup, one cabin competing against another.

They promised a special moonlight swim time just for this first night. That must have been what Francie was trying to tell me. The pool was twice the size of the one at the officers' club. At any other time, if I'd been offered a chance to swim in calm water at night, I would've been thrilled. But the pool stank of chlorine, and I couldn't find Francie in the crowd of at least a hundred kids.

When I finally bumped into her, she was paddling along in the middle of her *cool* Barbie-doll friends from Cabin Two. "Hi, Debbie. Isn't this fantastic?" And she moved on without even inviting me to stick with them.

Cabin Six seemed to have the quiet people. At dinner, I had liked Jill and Connie best, but it wasn't the same as being with Francie.

I wanted to go home.

Chapter 20:
Junior High

Ool means Deh-bee, Paw,
And Way will be gone all day.
At breakfast, I cry.

First day of school. First day of *junior high* school. Candi slouched against the outside wall of the bus stop shelter, looking like a blond Agent 99 from *Get Smart* in her sleek, plaid, way-too-short jumper. Rita and I arrived at the same time from opposite directions.

"Well, look at the next Miss Texas," Candi mimicked Rita's southern twang.

With her dimples and fringed shirt, Rita reminded me of Audra from the *Big Valley* television western.

"I'd be wearing that jumper if you hadn't seen it first." She wore a grin, but I was pretty sure Rita was jealous. Maybe she would figure out some day that she could have friends who were a lot nicer than Candi. Like me.

Rita scanned my red paisley dress, then nodded a

hint of approval. "Nice outfit. Where did you get it?"

"Grants." As soon as I'd tried on the dress, I knew it was mine. I felt as cute as Gidget the TV beach bunny. Even Krista seemed enthralled with it. All morning, she had followed me around wanting to use her finger to trace the red and black swirls.

Candi rolled her eyes. Grants was too cheapo for her.

"I bought it with my own money." I bet neither of *them* had earned money this summer.

"That's right. Your quaint little nursery school." Candi snickered.

Why was she always spoiling for a fight? When she turned that attitude on me, I usually let her blather on while I tuned her out.

Nothing she could say would make me feel bad about my "little nursery school." At the end of the four weeks, Angela had turned into a helper instead of a Miss Bossy, Terence entertained us at all the right times and cut it when I asked him to, and Sherri remained the sweetest little kid I ever met. I even taught the whole class several words in sign language, which made them the most educated preschoolers on the base.

Candi looked me up and down and raised her eyebrows.

Now what?

"Your mother let you buy that dress? It's a bit short, don't you think?"

I looked down at my bare knees. Miniskirts were all the rage, but the school wouldn't let us have hemlines that showed more than two inches above the knee. *My* hemline was fine.

Candi's jumper barely reached to mid-thigh. And

mine was a bit short? "You're the one who's in danger of getting sent home."

"Guess she told you." Rita snorted back a laugh as the bus rolled up spewing diesel fumes.

Candi glared at her, then at me, before she boarded.

The school bus deposited us at the brand-new junior-senior high school. Not only did the kids from two nearby villages join up with Hampton Shores, six different grades shared the school. An ocean of teenagers surged past me, while a handful of teachers stood like lighthouses as roiling waves of kids swirled around them. Candi and Rita were swept away in the commotion, not that they wanted my company or anything.

I was on my own. Again.

Six chalkboards had been set up in the front foyer, one for each grade. Each board listed room numbers with the beginning letters of last names next to them to indicate homerooms. The seventh-grade chalkboard stood on the far left. Room 103 indicated names between F and H. Which meant Mickey Hinkley was in my homeroom. *Great.* He'd kept his distance since last spring, but still. It would be awkward.

Everything smelled new as I walked down the hall, jostled by dozens of other wandering students. A hint of fresh paint on every wall. The aroma of never-used books. In spite of a thousand shoes tromping on the floors, the new tile still smelled soapy. Lockers lined the walls. Which one would be mine? Would I be able to remember the combination to unlock it?

Two tall guys brushed past me, then smacked the back of some poor little kid's head. The size of a nine-year-old, he was a prime target for bullies. Which reminded me. Jimmy Pulizzi was the new boy at some school in New York City. Were bullies after him? Or would he go back to being the toughest kid on his bus?

Room 103 was exactly where I expected to find it. Between 101 and 105. No teacher stood at this door, although other teachers chatted with students nearby. I stepped into my homeroom, its walls almost bare, not at all like my elementary school with its colorful bulletin boards and posters. The small cork board next to the door held one standard sheet of paper with some kind of list printed on it, and the back wall sported two posters that looked like travel advertisements to Spain and Mexico. I must be in the foreign language wing.

A class schedule lay on top of each desk, except these desks didn't have any place to hold books and supplies. They were more like little tabletops attached to chairs. The schedule on the desk nearest to the door belonged to somebody named Julian Fairmont. If Fs were on the hallway side of the room, then Hs must be near the windows. I moved toward the outside wall. First desk, two rows from the window. Cynthia Jane Hammond. She'd been in my fifth-grade class, but we weren't together last year.

Next desk. Charles Winthrop Handlon. Chip's real name was Charles? And *Winthrop?* Huh.

Next desk. Deborah Lynne Hansen. My name *really* appeared on a junior high schedule. It said my day started with New York History and ended with Spanish 1A. I *really* was old enough to take a foreign language. I was *really* going to change classes every hour. My heart pounded a drum roll of great expectations.

Marty Horvath plopped into the chair on my left. His hair had gotten almost as long as a rock star's. He picked up his schedule, glanced at it, and flipped the paper back on his desk. "And so it begins."

I waited for the punchline. Even the teachers laughed at Marty's antics—until he pushed it too far.

"Were you able to get your locker open?" he asked me.

"My locker?" How come he already had a locker and I didn't?

He pointed to the teacher's note on the chalkboard.

Please make sure your locker combination works before the bell rings. You'll find the combination on the top right corner of your schedule.

I grabbed my schedule and hurried to the hallway, now filled with the additional bedlam of lockers slamming and echoing down the corridor. Top right corner…sure enough…A137—26-9-53. I turned left and found A161 followed by A162. *Turn right, Debbie. Hurry up.* A137 turned out to be closer to Room 101 than my own homeroom. With shaky fingers, I spun the slippery plastic knob clockwise, like Mom had instructed. A couple of circles, then stop on 26. Counterclockwise one full circle, then stop on 9. Clockwise directly to 53. Oops, went right past it.

I scanned the hall for a clock. No clock. At least, several of us were still out here wrestling with our lockers. If the bell rang, I wouldn't be the only person who was late. Right 26, left 9, right 53. Click. The locker door opened. I *really* had a locker.

I was *really* in junior high school.

Chapter 21:
Sarah and Chip

Mah-mi knows I'm sad.
She gave me three oh-we-ohs.
She deserves a smile.

When I returned to the classroom, a girl I'd never seen before had claimed the desk to my right. She was short and petite, and her curly blond hair rippled all the way to her hips. I wished I could grow my hair that long. She stared at her schedule and bit her lip, looking as nervous as I felt.

Should I say something? I chickened out. I was no good at chitchat. When she looked up, though, I smiled at her. The wrinkle on her forehead smoothed out, but her lip was still held captive by her front teeth.

Encouraged, I gave chitchat a try. "Hi. I'm Debbie Hansen."

"I'm Sarah. Sarah Gulch."

"Nice to meet you." *Now what do I say?* "Are you from East Shore or Shinnecock?"

She shook her head. "I live in Hampton Shores, but

I went to St. John's through sixth grade."

No wonder she looked so nervous. I glanced around the classroom. "This is only the second place I've ever lived where I got to start school in the same town for two years in a row."

Her eyes widened. "Really? You had to change schools every year?"

"Nope. Sometimes, I had to change twice in one year. I went to two kindergartens, two first grades and two second grades."

She stared at me, speechless. Maybe I needed to change the subject. "What does your schedule look like? I placed my schedule on her desk. "Do we have any classes together besides homeroom?"

We compared the slips of paper as the classroom filled up with more students. Between Marty turning his desk into a bongo drum and voices shouting over one another, the two schedules did the talking for us. Yes. We had gym class together fourth period, and then fifth period English, which meant we'd have the same lunch hour. We smiled at each other in happy relief. Someone to sit with at lunch.

A motion near my side caught my attention. Chip set a spiral notebook on his desk. Then he placed his pen along one edge of the notebook.

. Before he could sit down, I stood up and grabbed a pencil from *my* desk. As I passed by him on the way to the pencil sharpener, I discovered I was at eye level with his shoulder, and I thought Francie had gotten tall. Last year, when we had to do square dancing, the top of Chip's head reached *my* shoulder.

By the time I returned from my unnecessary errand, Chip sat at his desk studying his schedule. My bashfulness kept the word "hi" stuck in my throat.

Marty cleared his. When I glanced his way, he wore a smirk with attitude, kind of like the way he wore his black T-shirt. Did he notice my surprise about how much Chip had changed? Was I that obvious?

Marty leaned back in his seat, arms behind his head. "Nice dress, Debbie. You look good in red."

My face probably matched the dress.

"Atención, clase."

I spun to face the blackboard at the unexpected tenor voice. A short, swarthy man stood behind the teacher's desk that held the nameplate "Señor DeLanza."

"Please be seated, and I will take the roll." His "will" sounded like *weel.* He lifted a sheet of paper from his desk. "Fairmont, *Hoolian*?"

While several kids snickered at the man's pronunciation of Julian, the kid at the front corner seat by the door said, "Here."

"Fansler, Mary?" Sr. DeLanza flipped the "r" in Mary so it came off as M*eddy.*

With a giggle, *Meddy,* behind Julian, raised her hand.

He continued until everyone was accounted for. Nobody fooled around. After roll call, we had to fill out six forms for stuff like emergency contacts and health records. By the time we were done, it was long past eight-forty, when we should've been in our first period class.

Sr. DeLanza glanced at the clock. "Today we are on a shortened schedule of classes. When you leave this room at nine o'clock, *peek* up the sheet with today's schedule. Lunch will be served during sixth period instead of fifth, and we will have a school assembly at two in the afternoon. Do you have any questions?"

From somewhere behind me, a male voice called out, "Do we go to lunch just before sixth period or just after?"

Sr. DeLanza raised one black eyebrow. "In future, I expect you to raise your hand *eef* you have a question."

The class turned their attention to the offender of the rule. I didn't know this boy either. Even after the rebuke, he kept an insolent grin on his face. He raised his hand, arm extended straight to the ceiling.

Sr. DeLanza nodded for him to speak.

"Mr. DeLuca, just before sixth period or just after?"

Sr. DeLanza studied the kid for a moment, then consulted his paper. "You are Mr. Gibson?"

"Yessir." The grin hadn't left his face.

The teacher pivoted and strode to the chalkboard. He wrote *A, B, C* in a vertical list. "*Eef* you will each consult your schedules, you will see that fifth period (*peddiod*) has a letter next to it. *Eef* you have an *A*, you will have the first lunch hour, *eef* you have a *B*, you have the second lunch hour, and *C* of course is last. *Eef* you have A Lunch, go directly to the cafeteria. Don't report to your class until after lunch. Those with B and C Lunches, the teacher will tell you when it is time to eat."

I studied my schedule. *5A.* So I should go to the cafeteria before I go to English. Well, thank you, *Mr. Gibson.* Sarah and I would've searched for the right classroom, and no one would've been in there.

A loud buzz from the intercom startled me, and I

dropped my schedule. It slid under Chip's chair.

Sr. DeLanza pointed to the clock. "That is your signal to dismiss from homeroom and go to your first *peddiod* class. Have a good day. *Buenos días*."

With the shuffling of papers, the scrape of chairs against the floor, and the clatter of a couple of dropped pencils, most kids shuffled out the door. But first, I had to retrieve my schedule. As I bent to reach for it, Chip leaned down for his pen lying on the floor next to my paper. We bumped heads.

"Whoa, sorry! I didn't see you."

I rubbed my forehead. "My fault. I should have said something to let you know I had to get under your chair."

I had to get under your chair? Sounded like I was going to huddle under there for a duck and cover drill in case the Soviet Union detonated a nuclear bomb over the school.

Chip retrieved my schedule and handed it to me. His green plaid button-down shirt looked great on him. "Where do you go first?"

"New York History."

"Me, too. Room 110?"

"Yeah."

"Shouldn't be too hard to find." He grinned.

By this time, the first period Spanish class was trickling into the room while Sr. DeLanza's finger wagged in the Gibson kid's face.

Chip grabbed his notebook from his desk. "Let's go."

He turned toward me again, and our eyes met. I'd never noticed that he had beautiful gray eyes. They reminded me of Smokey, the kitten I once had.

Mickey sauntered past us, a smirk on his face. "You two lovebirds are gonna miss your first class."

Red-faced, and without another word, we hurried from the room.

I liked it that we left the room together. I liked that a lot.

Chapter 22:
She Goes Where We Go

Pink stick on pink cake.
Mah-mi sets the stick on fire!
I can't eat burnt cake.

Mom had baked a strawberry-flavored cake with pink frosting. She had tied balloons to every chair at the dining room table. When she brought in the homemade cake with a lit candle on top, we turned off the lights and sang "Happy Birthday," which was kind of off-pitch except for Daddy and me.

"Blow out the candles," Mom said.

Krista looked at her but didn't move.

Mom pointed to the candles.

Krista looked at them. She seemed scared, and smart enough to know fire is hot.

I tapped her shoulder and pretended to blow out her candles. I hadn't learned the sign for that yet. Besides, the fact that Krista could use signs but not talk made Mom uncomfortable, which probably went back to our big fight last summer. She never told me to stop with the sign language, though.

Krista grinned at my charade for blowing out candles. She leaned closer and kind of breathed on them. All of us cracked up. She tried again. Same result. Wade joined her, and together, on the count of three, they blew on the candles. The flames disappeared, everyone cheered, and Krista looked pleased but puzzled.

With the lights back on, Mom served cake on teddy bear plates. Krista ate two slices of cake, although probably one of those slices remained on her face and the highchair tray.

"Mom, how did you know strawberry cake is Krista's favorite?" I asked. She's never said so." *She's never said anything.*

Mom kissed Krista's cheek and got a strawberry-cake kiss in return. "She goes shopping with me. I lined up all the flavors and had her pick one out."

Paul grinned at Krista's pink-frosted lips. "She sure knew what she wanted."

As soon as I hung up my jacket after school on the day Mom and Krista went to the doctor, I wandered into the kitchen.

"How was Krista's one-year check-up?"

Concentrating on paring a potato, Mom's head snapped up at my question and glared at me. I backed away. What did I say wrong? Or was this check-up worse than the one in April?

"I don't want to talk about it right now. Go read or

something."

It must've been really bad. I observed the mountain of potato peels. How many potatoes could one family eat? But I didn't ask what was for dinner. I might not want to know.

We sat down to a meal of mashed potatoes and canned tomato soup at the Formica kitchen table.

"Where's the grilled cheese?" Paul stretched his neck to search the counter for a platter of golden toast with melted cheese.

"We're having mashed potatoes instead." This from Mom.

Wade scooped a spoonful of white goop. "But we always have grilled cheese with tomato soup."

"Not tonight." This from Daddy.

Mashed potatoes suited me just fine. I hated grilled cheese. But these potatoes looked weird. Mom had put too much milk in them.

After a moment of glum silence, Wade asked with fake cheeriness, "Can I put my potatoes in my soup?"

Mom's forehead wrinkled into an expression of disgust, and then she shrugged. "Do what you want."

"Cool!"

"But don't get soup all over the table when you plop it in."

No problem. The potatoes slid off the spoon with hardly a splash into the orange pool. Paul joined Wade in the experiment, but I wasn't tempted. Milky or not, I loved the flavor of pure potatoes.

Krista didn't seem to mind them either. Mom fed her spoonful after spoonful and never touched her own plate.

Nobody talked. Had that ever happened before?

Dinner was always a time of kids talking over each other trying to grab Mom's or Dad's attention, but at the moment, I was sure Mom didn't care that I got an A on my science test. The boys seemed to know the highlights of their baseball practices wouldn't interest her either.

Paul pushed his empty bowl away from the edge of the table and asked, "May I be excused?" He started to rise from his chair.

"Not yet." Daddy directed a question to Mom. "Is Paul excused, or do you want us all to stay here while you tell us what happened at Dr. Winkler's?"

Mom's voice pierced the room like the crack of a rifle. I almost dropped the stack of bowls I was carrying to the sink. "The man told me to stuff Krista into some institution! He said we should concentrate on the three children we had and to let the state care for the fourth one who will most certainly regress."

I carefully lowered the dishes into the sink. "What's regress?" To send Krista away would be horrible. Was "regress" something worse?

The grim expression on Daddy's face added to my fear. "It means to go backwards. So he's saying Krista will only grow so much, then she will act more and more like a baby. She'll never grow up."

It took me a moment to understand. Paul was quicker and spit out the response I was still trying to put into words. "So, because she might always stay a baby, we should put her in a place where no one loves her and forget she ever existed? Who would do that to a baby?"

"That would be worse than when she was in the hospital!" Wade jumped from his chair and ran to Krista. He wrapped his arms around her as if that would protect her from evil doctors. She grinned at the unexpected love from her peskiest brother.

Paul wasn't done. "What kind of a doctor is this?"

"Not one I'm impressed with." Daddy's eyes never left Mom's across the table. "What else did the man have to say?"

"He wants another appointment in two weeks to discuss all of this further, and at that time he'll decide about the cataract in her eye." Mom set down her spoon. She hadn't had a drop of soup anyway. "And he told us to expect epileptic seizures and diabetes."

Heavy silence reigned over the table. Back in Syracuse, one of Mom's friends was epileptic. Sometimes, she would pass out and drop to the floor or end up lying on the ground stiff as a board and moaning. Scary.

Would such a horrible thing happen to Krista? And if it did, was that a good enough reason to send her away forever to rot in some lonely gray room until she eventually shriveled up and died?

Mom stroked the top of Krista's head. The baby, who'd been using one finger to shove drops of mashed potato into a variety of designs across the highchair tray, looked up and offered her an eight-toothed smile of pure joy.

Mom answered my unspoken questions. "This little one isn't going anywhere without the rest of us."

The boys and I looked Daddy's way. His face had softened, and he wore a wistful smile. "Of course not. She goes where we go."

Two weeks later, Mom let me skip school and go to the appointment. Daddy had refused to go with her. Since they'd already decided there would be no further discussion on institutions, he didn't see why he should miss work. But she was the one who had to face the doctor. So, she took me along. "For moral support," she said.

Mom still hoped to get a referral for an eye doctor. Not only did Krista have the cataract, her right eye also tended to roll toward her nose, making her cross-eyed on that side.

At the doctor's office, Krista relaxed on Mom's lap as she moved her head from side to side looking at all the shiny objects on his desk. There would be no physical exam, and she seemed to know that. Maybe because nobody took off her clothes and made her lie down on a cold, vinyl-covered table.

I sat in the chair next to them, nervous, and inhaling the weird combination of disinfectant spray and pipe tobacco. After two quick flicks of light into Krista's face from the beam of his mini-flashlight, Dr. Winkler leaned back in his chair. "A simple surgery could remove the cataract; a different operation can straighten the eye so it won't roll in, but there's no reason to bother."

"If a surgeon can fix it, it's definitely worth the bother," Mom said.

"Yes, but performing expensive procedures on a child with no prospects in life is a waste of your money."

Excuse me? Was this guy aware that he was talking to people who loved the adorable, little doll baby sitting across from him? With his wavy dark hair, he was almost as handsome as Ben Casey, but the TV doctor would never talk to his patients like that.

"You don't recommend surgery because Krista is mentally retarded?" Mom lifted her purse from the floor, gripping the handle so tightly, her knuckles turned white.

"There are excellent residential institutions that can take care of children like Krista." The man looked at her with pity and regret like, *I am so sorry you have a moron for a daughter. But that's the way it is.* "Van Wyck Manor, for instance. It's lovely. Close to Queens."

Van Wyck Manor? Sounded more like "Van Wicked Man" to me. My sister would be living near a *wicked man* over my dead body.

"This baby will not be going to any institution, no matter how *lovely.*" Mom handed me her purse, then the diaper bag. She stood with a jerk. Although she had a solid hold on Krista, the surprise move had the baby grabbing tightly around Mom's neck. "Retarded people deserve as much help as the rest of the world. If you won't assist in improving Krista's health, we'll find someone who will."

She swept out of his office like a queen exiting the throne room, and I, Princess Debbie, trailed behind her.

But before I walked out the door, I turned back, and with clear enunciation added the moral support Mom had brought me along for. "Your services are no longer required."

A choking sound came from the hall. Princess Debbie was probably in trouble.

Not sorry.

Chapter 23:
Goodbyes and Hellos

Hurray! No more ool.
Deh-bee is sad. Doesn't she
Want to play with me?

"Your services are no longer required." Mom used a high voice to mimic me once we were back in the car. "Oh, Debbie that was so rude." She covered her mouth with one hand, and her shoulders shook.

Oh, no. I'd made her cry.

"Your services are no longer—" Her high voice broke off, and a giggle erupted from behind her hand.

She wasn't crying. She was laughing.

I cracked a grin. "I know it was rude, but it's such a good line. I never thought I'd ever get to use it."

"Much classier than 'You're fired,'" she agreed. That remark sent her into another paroxysm of laughter.

Krista watched us with interest, joining us by adding a perky smile of her own.

I pointed to myself and tapped my nose twice. *I*

funny.

Mom suddenly sobered, her lips pressed into a thin line. She turned the key in the ignition, and we headed home.

So, I wasn't grounded for being rude to a doctor, and Sarah and I were still able to go to Chip's birthday party over the weekend.

On Monday morning, as I slid into my seat at homeroom just before the obnoxious buzzer sounded, Sarah looked my way, her eyes puffy and red. What could have happened between yesterday and now?

I leaned toward her and whispered, "What's the matter?"

Her lips turned down as she pressed them together. "I'll tell you at lunch."

The morning crept by. We experienced the oh-so-exciting thrill of listing products that were manufactured in New York between 1800 and 1850 as the Industrial Revolution gained speed. We had to write down why this was so important. I didn't know why. Wasn't the teacher supposed to tell me?

In math, Mr. Larraby divulged the wonders of base six. I knew our arithmetic was base ten. Why did we need to know base six? And base two? All you worked with were ones and zeroes. What could anybody do with that?

As we headed to fourth period science, I almost forgot about Sarah. Chip took my hand as we walked down the hall. He'd never held my hand before. It was warm and strong. Girls passed by us, then whispered to each other. Guys grinned and gave Chip a little lift of their chin.

What if he wanted me to eat lunch at his table? I'd have to tell him no. Sarah needed me. If I chose Sarah over him, would it ruin everything? But after class, Chip offered me a casual wave and went off with his buddies like usual.

Sarah chose a table away from the crowd of girls we usually sat with. I set down my tray complete with a hamburger, fries, and a carton of juice, then ignored it and waited for Sarah to say something.

Her round blue eyes shimmered with tears. With all those gold ringlets shrouding her shoulders and the terrible sadness surrounding her, she reminded me of Rapunzel trapped in the tower.

"My mom told me we're moving to Florida over Christmas break."

No wonder she was in tears. I joined her. It had been so good to have a friend after Nancy left, and now I'd be alone again. Sarah had finally gotten comfortable in a new school, and she'd have to begin all over again. I knew the feeling too well. It wasn't so bad when I was little, but once a person reaches junior high, finding new friends is like auditioning for a role in a hundred movies before you finally land a walk-on part.

What could I say to make her feel better? What could make *me* feel better? Nothing. The decision had already been made. "Why does your mom want to move?"

She picked up a napkin and wiped her eyes. "You know my parents got divorced last spring, which is why I had to change schools."

I nodded. "Your mom didn't have money for

private school anymore, and your dad wouldn't pay for it."

"Yeah." She sighed. "I understood why Mom couldn't afford the school. But now she says she can't afford living up here. She makes her money during tourist season, and it's not enough to take us through the winter." She blew her nose into the napkin. "At least, that's what she claims."

"Doesn't your dad have to pay alimony or something?"

"She says that's still not enough for our expenses."

"Florida must be expensive, too," I argued.

"Yeah, but she can work year-round at the beach restaurants down there."

"Oh."

There was nothing more to talk about. A cloud of depression hovered directly over our heads while the rest of the cafeteria enjoyed lunch in the sunshine.

I helped Sarah pack up her bedroom on the first day of Christmas vacation.

"I wish I could go with you," I said. "You're going to have a year-round tan."

"I burn. I don't tan." Sarah wasn't about to accept any encouragement from me.

"But you'll be warm. I'm always freezing in the winter, even inside."

"Let Chip keep you warm." She cracked a smile.

I threw a sock at her. "I wish."

What else could I say to make her feel better? I was the one who had moved a gazillion times. What had made me fine with it? Well, I'd always had my whole family. All Sarah had was her mom.

"Sarah?"

"Mmm?" She filled a box with the knickknacks from her dresser.

"Remember the first day of school?"

"Mm-hm."

"Remember how I told you I'd been the new kid lots of times?"

"Mm-hm."

"Were you glad that I talked to you that first day?"

"Yeah." She looked up from the box she'd been concentrating on.

"Well, when you go to school that first day, if nobody talks to you, look for someone who's shy, who isn't talking to anyone in homeroom."

She stared at me.

"And go over to her and introduce yourself. Tell her you're new. Babble about where you come from and why you had to move, if you have to."

Sarah resumed her packing. "What does that have to do with anything?"

"That person might become your first friend at the new school."

She met my gaze. "That easy, huh?"

"Sometimes." I nodded with years of experience to back me up. How come I didn't follow my own advice? "Sometimes, it's that easy."

While Sarah and her mom traveled to her grandma's house in New Jersey on Christmas Eve, I went to the candlelight service at church. While she opened gifts with two lonely ladies, I enjoyed a big family dinner with cousins and watched Krista play in all the wrapping paper. On the twenty-sixth, while Sarah took to the road for sunny Florida, I played silly games with Krista and her favorite toy giraffe. I built a small igloo with my brothers. I won all the canasta games with Grandma.

Underneath it all, I knew Sarah was gone.

Mom and Daddy stowed the last-minute items while I shivered on the stiff, vinyl seat inside the frigid station wagon. At four-thirty in the morning, they worked in silence so as not to wake the neighbors. The only lights to guide them shone from above the garage door and inside the car. The boys and I were under strict orders to talk in whispers, but every thump of a suitcase, every door gently shut, echoed across the neighborhood in the icy stillness of the night.

No matter where we traveled, Daddy always chose to drive through New York City before dawn, so he'd miss rush hour traffic. I didn't mind. The sooner we left, the sooner we'd get to our Christmas Vacation Destination—Upstate New York. I would get to see Francie. We'd skate at Green Lakes and go sledding on really steep hills.

Hampton Shores didn't have steep sledding hills, and ice was rarely thick enough to hold our weight. We only skated on shallow ponds. That way, if we fell through, we just got soaked to the knees and climbed out. The boys always kept playing hockey. I went home to get dry and warm.

Visiting Francie would be the best, the icing on the cake, a sundae with whipped cream and a cherry on top, and we were saving the best for last. So first, we were going to Plattsburgh to visit Mom's Cousin Lynne. The only things I remembered about her were red hair, aqua eyes, and she was funny and loud.

Paul had called dibs on the cubbyhole space in the back of the station wagon. I wanted to "sit on the hump" next to the car seat where I could watch over Krista, so Wade started out on my left sitting behind Daddy. We would rotate seats every two hours.

I loved road trips.

Except my teeth were chattering because Daddy hadn't turned on the engine to warm up the car yet. I burrowed into my heavy coat, letting my breath warm my face, which had the effect of a drizzling rain. Just like I'd learned in science class, the air I breathed out condensed immediately onto the cold wool, and my nose rested against those water droplets. Ugh. It felt like I had a runny nose.

Daddy stepped on the open door frame on the driver's side to cinch the tarp over the suitcases on the roof. Mom opened the front passenger door and handed me the diaper bag which I placed on the floor in front of the car seat. Then she passed me a bag filled with snacks. "Put this next to Krista's stuff."

With clumsy, mittened fingers, I squeezed the food in next to it. There.

Mom nodded and hopped in the car, closing her door with barely a click against the sub-freezing temperatures. She planted a gigantic purse on the bench seat between her and Daddy, set the thermos of coffee on the floor to the left of her feet, and stuffed an empty paper bag between her seat and the door.

A last gust of wind needled my face as Daddy pulled shut the driver's side. "Ready?" He turned the key in the ignition and looked at us, waiting for any last-minute bathroom runs or "I forgots."

Paul, wrapped in his sleeping bag, feet against the "entertainment" box, gave a thumbs-up. Wade nodded.

"Ummmm, Daddy?" I looked at the empty car seat.

"What did you forget, Debbie?"

"I think we forgot Krista. She's not here."

Mom shrieked a prayer to the Almighty as she flung open her door and ran for the house. A light flicked on in Mrs. Gaston's window. So much for not waking the neighbors.

Chapter 24:
Winter Road Trip

Blanket. Dark. Cold. Car.
I will sleep on the long trip.
I smile at Deh-bee.

By the time Mom returned with a blanket-bundled package, the car had warmed to mild spring temperatures. Paul had removed his coat and Wade's was unzipped. I remained fully wrapped but had taken off my mittens. Still too cold, I sat on my hands.

Krista made sleepy little moans while Mom strapped her into the seat. For a moment, she opened her eyes and offered me a half smile, but as soon as the car moved, the baby drifted back into slumber.

Our journey to the Frozen North had begun.

The first hours in the dark car were peaceful. The thud-thud of tires as they rolled over the seams in the road almost lulled us back to sleep, but Paul, Wade, and I never slept in the car. We didn't play games. There wasn't enough light to read by. We simply looked at the stars, and eventually, the sunrise.

Winter road trips weren't as much fun as when we traveled in the summer. Who wants to eat on a snow-covered picnic table? No place to take a break and run around outside for long. It was too cold. But we savored a sense of risky adventure. What if ice covered the roads? What if we got stuck in a blizzard? Could we survive on cookies and crackers?

One time we were driving on the New York Thruway, and it snowed so hard Daddy rolled his way on the white-pack carpet like a blind man tapping his cane on the sidewalk. A huge drift crossing the highway stopped us completely. We couldn't see past it.

"I'm going through," Daddy said.

"What if we hit something on the other side?" Mom argued, her voice rising in volume.

He was even louder. "There's no one else on the road, Dorothy. We can't just sit here."

He backed up the car and revved the engine. Mom pressed her lips together and said nothing further. The boys and I looked at each other, silent. Daddy gunned it.

I squeezed my eyes shut, grabbed Wade's hand, and said a prayer in my head. I opened my eyes just as we hit the white wall.

White, white, white. And then we broke through. The snow still fell fast, but we could see the path of some snowplow that had passed by a little earlier.

Paul bounced up and down in his seat. "That was so cool!"

Wade didn't perform his usual role of Paul's echo. He stayed silent and wouldn't release his death grip on my hand. Once my heartbeat slowed down, though, I kind of agreed with Paul. We had rammed through a mountain of snow and survived, almost as exhilarating as when Meg, the main character in *A Wrinkle in Time,* tessered through the universe.

No such adventure waited for us on this trip. No winter storms predicted, and definitely no cruising across the cosmos. The hint of dawn glowed orange, then yellow. By the time the sun peeked over the horizon, the day promised cloudless skies. We wouldn't see one snowflake.

The Catskill Mountains surrounded us in mounds of gray and white in the dim light, a lot different from their summer greens when Francie and I were at camp. We'd talked on the phone a few times since then, and I'd forgiven her for that moonlight swim snub. She hadn't even known I was mad at her. I wished I could be more like Francie or Nancy, outgoing and friendly to everyone.

Mom poured from the thermos and handed a cup to Daddy. A blend of coffee aroma and stale cigar smoke filled the car. While I loved how pipes smelled when the match first hit the tobacco, cigars always stank. There had to be something unhealthy about that stuff.

Krista slept almost to Albany, waking up once the sunlight streamed through her window. Mom handed me a teething biscuit to give to her. She sucked on the cookie and squinted, peering out the window. Not much to see besides sky and rounded mountain tops.

As we approached the more rugged Adirondack Mountains, the boys and I rotated seats again. I fished around for Krista's favorite stuffed giraffe and gave it to her before I climbed into the back cubbyhole, finally peeling off my coat and adding it to the pile behind

Krista.

Paul moved from the middle hump to behind the driver's seat. "Give me the pad and a pencil, Debbie."

I plucked the items from our entertainment box and tossed them to him.

He wrote his name at the top of the first sheet of paper. "Are you gonna play the car game with us?"

"Nope. I'm going to read my book."

Without my asking, Wade leaned down, picked up my book from under his dangling feet, and dropped it over the back of the seat. So while Mom oohed and aahed over the scenery of grim, rugged mountains, the boys watched for Chevrolets and Fords, marking tallies upon each sighting. I inhaled the perfume of ink on paper and sank into the story of *Shadow Castle.*

Just as Prince Mika snatched his son from the evil goblins and sprinted out of the cave, a familiar voice buzzed from the distance like a fly landing on a hot light bulb. A rough shake to my shoulder jolted me out of my book world.

"Debbie!" Paul glared at me and jabbed my shoulder again.

I flinched. "Stop it."

He knelt on the seat, facing backward, and held out a Pop Tart in the hand that hadn't attacked me. "Mom said to stop reading and eat."

"*Okay.*" I wiggled out of my cocoon in the cubby hole and sat upright. "You didn't have to poke me."

"Jeepers, what was I supposed to do? I called you three times."

To make sure he knew I was irritated, I whipped my hair around hoping it would slap him in the face.

He leaned back, so all I slapped was the Pop Tart.

Now I had crumbs in my hair.

He dropped the Pop Tart in my lap, his expression daring me to escalate our conflict into all-out war.

"Debbie. Paul. Enough." Dad's voice, but Mom's face turned in our direction held just as much grim warning. Daddy hated sweeping out crumbs after a trip. Paul and I probably just earned the job.

I saw Krista had drifted off again, her giraffe snuggled between Wade and the car seat. How could she sleep in the car like that? Especially with Paul yelling at me? She had to be deaf.

But deafness wouldn't keep her from walking. At fifteen months old, she could stand on her tiptoes if she held onto furniture, but she couldn't stay balanced if she stood alone. Of course, if I never put my feet flat on the ground, I couldn't balance all that well either.

Chapter 25:
Cousin Lynne

A crazy stranger,
Too many hugs and kisses.
Go away, stranger.

By midafternoon, after two bathroom stops and lunch at a restaurant, we arrived at Cousin Lynne's. She swooped down on us as soon as we pulled into the circular driveway fronting her colonial brick home.

"Dorothy!"

As Mom swung her feet out of the car, Cousin Lynne yanked her to a standing position and wrapped her in a huge hug.

Lynne didn't wear a coat, only a cream-colored fisherman sweater, a turquoise scarf, and black ski pants, but she didn't seem to feel the ten-degree temperature. Paul and I slid out the driver's side while Wade climbed over the seat from his turn in the cubbyhole. Even though the air barely stirred, the tip of my nose still burned from the cold.

Before us lay a winter scene fit for a Christmas card. Pure white snow surrounded the dark bricks. Fir trees lined up like soldiers along one edge of the property. On the other side, leafless deciduous trees stood with branches wide and welcoming as if they were attending a lawn party.

I liked that word, *deciduous*. We'd learned about *deciduous* in science class last year. Conifers stayed green all the time, but deciduous trees couldn't *decide* what to wear, if anything. Green in spring and summer, a variety of colors in the fall, then shamelessly naked all winter. A single, bright-red cardinal perched in one of them.

Paul gazed across the broad yard. "Whoa! We can make a *giant* fort with all this."

Wade joined him. "Yeah, a *giant* fort." He turned a full circle. "And a million snowballs."

Paul grinned at him. "It's gonna be a great war."

A crow cawed from somewhere in the pine trees during the momentary silence while Cousin Lynne took a breath. As the boys and I rounded the hood of the car, she bore down on all three of us.

"*Debbie!* You're so *tall.* A young *lady.* And *boys!* You're not little *squirts* anymore."

I found myself smushed against her chest, struggling to breathe without inhaling wool fuzzies. Cousin Lynne was bigger than Mom. Not fat. Just big. Larger than life. Her shoulders were broad, her face square, and my memory was accurate when it came to her eyes. Aqua, like water in a swimming pool.

She let me go so abruptly I almost fell over.

"Oh, the *baby!*" She spun toward Mom again, who had removed Krista from her car seat.

Cousin Lynne lifted her, along with three blankets, from Mom's arms. When they were nose to nose, she shouted into the baby's face. "You are so *precious.*"

Krista's eyes opened wide. She leaned backwards and turned her head searching for Mom, who smiled reassurance. The poor little kid squirmed under her blankets trying to get away from this crazy lady.

Cousin Lynne got the message. "Oh, you are a *mommy's girl.*" Before Krista started to cry, Lynne dropped her into Mom's arms.

"Let's get all of you *in*side. I'll bet you're no longer used to this kind of *cold.* Bring in the bags, now. I'll show you where *everybody* is going to sleep." She shooed us inside like a sheepdog driving the flock into its pen. The men carried the biggest suitcases. The boys dragged in the smaller ones. I was assigned the diaper bag and all of my books.

We spent Wednesday piling on layers of clothing and peeling them off, building snowmen, having a snowball fight, and coming in for hot chocolate. Even Krista scooted around in the snow, and the boys and I took turns pushing her around on a plastic saucer. She giggled when we spun her in circles. Once it stopped, she put her mitten fingertips together. *More.*

One time, Wade spun her too hard, and she flipped off the side, face first into the snow.

I ran to pick her up. "You better not have hurt her."

He ran for her, too. Together, we rolled her over. Drops of melted snow on her face sparkled in the sunlight. Her eyes were closed.

"Did she drown in the snow?" Wade trembled. He looked from Paul and me to the house.

Should we call for help? Mom would kill us if we

hurt this baby. All three of us hovered over Krista. She couldn't have breathed in melted snow that fast, could she?

Krista's eyes popped open as our bodies shaded her face. Was she hurt? Would she scream?

She giggled and raised her arms for someone to pick her up. Wade hogged the honors. As soon as he hoisted her to his chest, she pointed at the saucer. *Again.* She couldn't say the word, didn't know the sign, but her meaning was clear.

Did Van Wyck Manor let their residents sled down hills? Of course not. Look what Krista would be missing. Stupid doctors and their recommendations. I tossed those thoughts out of my mind like throwing litter out of the car window and returned to the fun.

This time I sat on the saucer with Krista between my legs. If we flipped out in a spin, I could get us upright in no time. We did it again and again and again, spinning faster and faster, each of us taking turns holding Krista. Every once in a while, we sat her by herself and slowed the saucer way down. No sense in getting in trouble with Mom.

By late afternoon, I was content to sit next to the fireplace, sharing a sofa with Daddy on one end and me and my book on the other. Our sofa touched corners with the sofa where Mom and Cousin Lynne sat. Then the far corner of the second sofa met with one of two chairs facing me and Daddy. The whole thing created a cozy U in front of the fireplace.

Grown-up chat droned in my ears. While Cousin Lynne didn't know the meaning of the word *quiet*, her husband rarely spoke at all. The term "opposites attract" sure proved true in their case.

Henry was a professor at the local university. He and Daddy seemed to enjoy each other's company as they puffed on their pipes. Krista played with her beloved giraffe on the braided rug between Henry's chair and my sofa. Such a relaxing scene.

Until I realized they were all discussing plans for Thursday.

"Lake Placid isn't too far from here," Henry explained. "They've got a beautiful lodge with tobogganing, ice skating, and skiing."

"We should have brought our skates with us," Mom said.

"The only room to stow them would've been our laps." Daddy pointed toward the window where we could see the boys wrestling in the snow. "With those two, it might have been a dangerous drive."

I pictured them clobbering each other with the blades of their skates.

Cousin Lynne brought our attention back to Lake Placid. "Henry's a *fabulous* skier." She smiled at him in adoration. "But he'll be *happy* to go with you to the beginner slopes, if that's what the *kids* need."

We had to ski? I got nervous sledding down the small hills on Long Island.

Cousin Lynne wasn't finished. "Dorothy and I can stay in the lodge with the *baby*."

"I can stay in the lodge, too," I chimed in.

"Oh, it's kind of *boring* if you have to sit there all *day*."

Mom added, "You go with the boys. It'll be fun."

I stared at her. She stared back. Her one eyebrow lifted, and I dropped my eyes to my lap.

Right. It will be fun.

Even though we'd lived in Syracuse for two years, none of us had ever tried skiing. If I could barely wobble across a frozen pond on ice skates, I would probably kill myself on skis. The next time Francie saw me would be at my funeral.

Chapter 26:
Ski Trip

Sit on the circle.
Spin on the snow round and round
Or slide down the hill.

Cousin Lynne hallooed up the stairs to my attic bedroom long before dawn. *"Up and at 'em! I've got sausage and pancakes on the griddle,* and we have to get ready for *Whiteface Mountain."*

I could smell the spice of sausage two stories up but snuggled under the goose down comforter. So warm. On the floor below, the pounding of feet signaled that my brothers got the message. Another set of footsteps approached on the narrow attic stairs.

"Hey, sleepyhead." Daddy's hand gently nudged my shoulder.

I poked my nose out from under the comforter. *Brrr.*

"Did you sleep, okay? It's pretty chilly up here."

I yawned. "It was perfect."

"Good." He pulled the comforter away from my

head, and I tried to grab it back. "Nope," he said, "Get up, get dressed, and get downstairs."

"We're really going skiing?"

"Yup. It takes an hour to get to Lake Placid, so by the time we've had breakfast and pack up for the day, it's going to be late morning before we can get on the mountain."

"Do I have to go?"

"Debbie."

I heard his disappointment.

"Okay. Okay." I threw off the comforter and shivered in my flannel nightgown. "Two minutes."

He kissed my forehead. "See you in two minutes."

It only took one minute to speed change into long johns, ski pants, an undershirt, sweater, and two pairs of socks. This attic might receive weak puffs from the furnace through its vents, but now I knew how Laura Ingalls felt in her unheated loft bedroom from *The Little House on the Prairie.*

The agenda for the day was to ski, each according to his—or her--ability for a couple of hours, beginners on the bunny hill, experts on the black diamond runs. I guessed Henry would get us started on the "little" hill and eventually ski by himself on the more challenging slopes. We'd have some lunch at the lodge, and then everybody would stay together on the toboggan runs for the rest of the afternoon.

Once Henry demonstrated how to put on our skis, the plan fell apart, at least for me. My fingers fumbled on the thingamajiggits that would clamp my boots onto the skis. I looked around for assistance, and the wind bit into my face. Skiers glided down the slope. Others whooshed by on their way to the ski lift. Everyone was having fun. Not me. Even the baby bunny slope looked deadly. It was steeper than any sledding hill at home, and its snow was slick.

A film played in my head, going faster and faster with each rewind. Me performing a series of uncontrolled cartwheels down the incline, taking out a few toddlers on my way to the bottom and landing in a painful, undignified heap. *I* would never be graceful enough to slalom my way down a mountain. *I* would never laugh in delight, clambering back onto the T-bar to do it again. No, *I* was about as much fun as Eeyore on a day of sunshine and flowers in the Hundred Acre Wood.

Why couldn't I be like everyone else and look at that mountain as a challenge to conquer? I had faced down the biggest bully on the bus. I had picked myself up and soldiered on after losing Francie *and* Nancy *and* Sarah. I had survived and conquered when it came to dealing with my sister's heart surgery, and I was prepared to do whatever it took to help her. But skiing? I was a total loser.

Daddy, Henry, Paul and Wade stood in the sunshine, skis strapped on perfectly, eager to join the crowds who also exulted in the sunny day. I was the only one who sat in the shadow of the ski-rental shack, still unattached to the narrow blades under my feet.

I couldn't do this. I just couldn't. My choices were bad and worse. I could hold everyone else back, irritating them with my total lack of ability, or I could save myself public humiliation and not try. And then everyone would be disappointed in me. A wimp of a sister. A disappointment as a daughter. An ungracious guest. Fat tears rolled down my cheeks.

Daddy sighed. "We're supposed to enjoy a fun day, Debbie." He pointed to the lodge. "Skiing isn't supposed to make you miserable. Go find Mom."

Paul gave me a look of scathing contempt. Who wanted a crybaby for an older sister? Wade patted my back in sympathy, but he'd go wherever Paul led no matter how scared he might be. Henry turned toward the slopes, and the Hansen males followed.

I was such a failure.

Mom didn't appear surprised when I trudged into the commons room of the lodge, but Cousin Lynne's eyebrows rose past her auburn bangs. *"Debbie!"*

Great. Now the entire population of Whiteface Mountain would know what a coward I was.

Mom placed a hand on Lynne's arm and shook her head, and Lynne said nothing more until I reached their broad wingback chairs in front of the fire.

She asked in a whisper, "Are you okay? Did you get hurt?" Those aqua eyes scanned me up and down as if she were checking for blood seeping out from my layers of clothing.

If I talked, I'd cry again.

Mom sat Krista on Lynne's lap and motioned for me to come closer. "You got scared?"

I nodded.

She pulled me down beside her on the chair and wrapped a comforting arm around my waist. "I'll tell you a secret," she murmured into my ear. "I am so glad that I *had* to take care of Krista for the day. Great excuse not to ski."

"You would've been scared, too?"

"Petrified. I'm a born klutz."

"No, you're not. You can skate backwards."

Mom responded with smug smile. "Well, I *am* a good skater, but that's about it."

"I'm a klutz at skating, too."

"But you're a good dancer. I was so bad in tap class that once Grandpa saw me in a recital, he refused to pay for any more lessons."

Laughing, I peered into her face to see if she was lying. "He did not."

"He did. My feelings would have been hurt except I hated dance lessons, so I was more relieved than upset."

Cousin Lynne shook her head in disbelief. "I can't believe you're afraid to ski. On a *bunny* hill?"

At least she spoke quietly.

"How come *you're* not out there?" The question popped out of my mouth before I realized how rude my tone of voice must've sounded to a grown-up.

Her eyes widened for a moment before she answered, and Mom's hand around my waist squeezed my ribs. Hard.

"I figured your mom would want some company." Cousin Lynne suppressed a smile. "And…. Henry doesn't want me to ski this winter because… I'm going to have a *baby!*"

She couldn't suppress that voice.

Mom jumped from the chair with a little scream, almost tipping me out in the process. "Why didn't you say so before? We've been here for *three days.*"

Lynne stood, too. "It's so early in the pregnancy, I was afraid to say anything, but I couldn't stand keeping the *secret* any *longer.*"

They hopped and hugged in front of the fire with Krista in between them. In case the skiers who watched the spectacle thought I belonged with Mom and Cousin Lynne, I sidled over to the opposite wall and pretended to choose a board game from one of the shelves.

The crazy ladies finally settled back in their chairs with Krista cuddled on Cousin Lynne's lap once again. My sister might have considered her rather alarming in the beginning, but she was completely at home resting against her chest in this cozy lodge.

Cousin Lynne planted a smackaroo kiss on top of her head. "I hope my baby will be as calm and adaptable as this little sweetheart."

Unless the baby took after its father, her kid would deafen the neighborhood. Mom and Cousin Lynne spent the next hour talking maternity clothes and childbirth while I took Krista and ambled over to the picture window facing the black diamond slope. Dots of color from a hundred skiers' parkas glided down the mountain. Henry was in all black, and I saw plenty of dark dots among the brighter hues.

At noon sharp, Daddy, in his regular snow boots, tromped through the main doors of the lodge. He stepped over to the hearth and glanced up at the timbered ceiling appreciatively.

"Nice place." Warming his hands in front of the fire, he admired the wood-framed oil paintings on the walls, each depicting a different season in the Adirondacks.

I liked the spring painting the best. The trees showed off new-green leaves, and white blossoms on bushes promising warmer weather ahead. It probably took until late May for the mountain to grow that kind of color. I doubted I'd ever visit at that time of year. School didn't get out until a month after that.

"Where are the boys?" Mom asked.

"They're with Henry. I moved on to the blue square hill."

Blue was for intermediate skiers. For a first-timer, Daddy must be pretty good.

Cousin Lynne laughed. "Henry stayed on the bunny hill all this time?"

Daddy's eyes shifted to Mom and back to Cousin Lynne. "No, I left them on the green circle slope. The beginner level."

"They didn't stay on the baby slope for their first-time skiing?" Mom's voice rose in alarm.

I returned to the fireplace and pulled up a spare chair from another grouping. "Paul and Wade probably got bored with the bunny hill." No need for Mom to light into Daddy when we all knew what my brothers were like.

A couple of minutes later, Henry joined us. He grinned at Lynne, leaned over, and gave her a big kiss.

"I told Dorothy about the baby." Her eyes sparkled like a tropical sea in the sunlight.

Mom didn't care about the new baby anymore. "Where are Paul and Wade?"

"They wanted one more run. They'll be here in about five minutes."

It was more like ten, but then they burst in, skis and all.

"Whoa!" Daddy and Henry both strode across the room and ushered them back out. "Skis stay outside."

While Daddy returned the skis, the boys ran back inside. Their words tumbled over each other like rapids in a river as they told Mom about their morning.

"That was so cool."

"We started out on the stupid bunny hill."

 "Then we went to the easy slope."

"The green."

"After Dad left, we followed him to the blue hill."

"That was harder."

"But we didn't fall."

"Then Uncle Henry said it was time for lunch."

"But we wanted to go down one more time."

"So he said okay."

"He said he'd meet us at the lodge."

"So we found the black diamond and tried it."

"What?" Mom interrupted.

"Yeah, Wade went flying over this bump, and he almost made it, but he fell over when he landed."

"I was okay, though. It didn't even hurt."

"It was really steep the rest of the way. It was like driving a race car downhill."

"When's lunch?"

"Yeah, I'm starving."

But Mom was no longer listening. Her glare could've smoked tall, skinny Henry into a strip of beef jerky. "You let beginning skiers go down the expert hill?"

"I thought they were going down the blue hill. They'd already proved they could do it." He turned toward his wife for support, but Lynne wasn't smiling either.

Daddy rejoined us. One look at Mom's face, and he asked, "What happened?"

So the boys told their story again, this time with even more embellishment.

"Grant, I'm sorry." Henry hung his head like an overgrown puppy who'd chewed up the master's socks.

"I should've stayed with them."

The boys continued to beam over their accomplishments. Daddy's eyes twinkled.

"No harm done." He slapped Henry's shoulder but kept his eyes on Mom. "So you're going to be a dad? Congratulations."

Mom's expression was still angry, but she received Dad's message loud and clear. *Stop fussing.*

After a lunch of chili dogs and French fries, we rented two toboggans and spent the rest of the afternoon sledding. Even Krista and Mom got to go. Since we were sitting only an inch off the ground, Henry was okay with Lynne joining us, too.

Tucked in between Mom and Paul, I felt as safe as a baby bird in its nest. Besides, tipping over in a toboggan was a lot less scary than tumbling down a hill on skis. If we ever came back here, I'd spend the whole day on the toboggan hill.

Chapter 27:
Storm Clouds

Our food is stinky.
Deh-bee cries. Da-di red face.
Big noise. It scares me.

On Friday morning, the aroma of bacon made its way up two flights of stairs. No one needed to force me out of bed. This was Happy Reunion Day with Francie, and then two *more* days to spend together before traveling home.

I hopped out from under the comforter and speed-changed into corduroys and a sweater. Except for my toothbrush, I threw everything in the suitcase before running downstairs. After all that rush, I was still the last one getting to the large country kitchen.

An oddly silent room greeted me, the only sound coming from Cousin Lynne's metal spoon clanking against the iron skillet where she scrambled a panful of eggs. Henry read the newspaper and wore his professor clothes. Apparently, university professors worked during everyone else's vacations.

I should've walked into lots of talk from the boys about yesterday's great skiing and tobogganing and how they couldn't wait to get to Vinnie's house and build a snow fort like they used to do. Mom should be saying what a wonderful hostess Lynne had been and how much she'd miss her. Cousin Lynne should be booming her joy at having company and getting to see our new addition of Krista. Instead, the boys sipped orange juice and Mom stared at Daddy, who looked awfully glum for a man who loved to drive long distances.

No, this was more than *oddly* silent.

The oven door creaked as Cousin Lynne pulled out a plate piled high with toast and gently placed it on a potholder on the table. Her volume level was set on low. "Who likes their eggs *soft*?"

The boys raised their hands, and Mom nodded yes for herself. Daddy didn't seem to hear. Cousin Lynne stepped back to the stove and shoveled some eggs onto three dishes with a metal spatula.

"You like them *dry*, Debbie?"

"Yes, please."

Eggs are slimy. I'd rather have eggs that can bounce off the floor than have a glob of egg white somewhere in the mix.

She filled two more plates and set one in front of Henry and one at the empty place for herself. Mine would keep cooking. "Grant?" A pause. *"Grant?"* Volume control up.

Daddy frowned and lifted his head.

"Eggs?" Cousin Lynne asked.

"Yeah, sure."

This was getting too weird. Daddy *loved* breakfast.

He should've been singing an ode to the Golden Treasures of Scrambled Eggs.

Lynne showed me the fry pan with the last of the eggs in it. "Okay?"

I spied a shiny squiggle of white. "Could you cook it a little more?"

Mom rolled her eyes. "For heaven's sake, Debbie. Don't make Lynne do more work just for you."

"I don't mind." Cousin Lynne turned back to the stove.

"I can finish cooking them," I offered. "That way yours won't get cold."

"Aren't you a sweetheart?" She handed me the spatula. "Dorothy, you have such well-behaved children. You're going to have to tell me your secret so mine can be just as wonderful."

Usually, the boys grinned at each other like they were sharing a good joke when they heard that kind of compliment. But they didn't crack a smile.

Not able to stand the mystery any longer, I leaned toward Paul and whispered, "What is the matter with everybody?"

"We're not going to Syracuse. That's what's the matter." His voice boomed in the quiet kitchen.

What? Mom and Daddy wouldn't go back on their word. Mom wanted to see Francie's mom as much as I wanted to see Francie.

"Are the Capellis meeting us somewhere halfway?"

I knew the answer before I finished speaking. Why would both families spend lots of money on hotels when Francie's house had enough room for all of us?

Wade answered out loud. "No. They're staying in

Syracuse, and we're driving home. All because of some stupid snowstorm."

The nasty odor of burning eggs reached my nose. As soon as I'd heard the words, "No Syracuse," I'd forgotten all about them. I spun to the stove and started scraping the pan. The egg whites were dry enough *now*.

Mom and Cousin Lynne joined me. Mom grabbed for the spatula. "Oh, Debbie, this is a mess. All because you wanted them cooked more."

I refused to relinquish the spatula, pulled it forcibly from her grasp, and returned to my vicious scraping. "Don't worry. I'll eat what I burned."

Cousin Lynne placed a hand on my shoulder. "You don't have to do that."

Whether she meant I didn't have to eat the eggs or I didn't have to keep cleaning up my mess, I didn't care. I shrugged off her hand. "Yes, I do."

I would clean the stupid pan until every black speck was removed, and I would eat burnt eggs until I puked. The day couldn't get any worse.

Cousin Lynne silently returned to her seat.

Mom hissed into my ear. "You apologize to Lynne this instant."

"No."

The sound of metal against metal intensified as I dug in harder. With grim satisfaction, I rolled back an inch-wide ribbon of black across the bottom of the skillet.

Mom seized my wrist before the spatula could descend into the pan again.

I wrenched away. "Leave me alone. I made the mess. I'll clean it."

Daddy's hand slammed on the table, and I turned

with a startled hop.

"Deborah Lynne."

Six pairs of eyes shifted between me and Daddy. The sharp crack of his palm against the wood had roused Henry from his paper. Krista's face crumpled at Daddy's angry expression, and she set up a wail. I wanted to howl, too. I ran out of the kitchen, back up the stairs to my frozen room, and dove under the covers. I bet Lynne didn't think all of her cousin's children were so well-behaved now.

As I sobbed inside my goose down cave, footsteps sounded on the stairs. Daddy. It was always Daddy who could calm me down. He sat on the edge of the bed, his weight causing the mattress to sink so I rolled toward him. His hand explored the covers until it rested on my head.

"You're disappointed."

I said nothing, but my tears slowed down, and I tried to take deep breaths so I would stop shuddering.

He didn't expect an answer. "We're all disappointed." He patted my head. "But you know every time we travel in winter, it's a risk. Plans might change."

I sat up abruptly. "We travel in snow all the time. In storms, too. Remember when we drove through the giant snow drift? We didn't change our plans."

"That blizzard caught us by surprise. If I'd known the roads were going to be so bad, we wouldn't have started out."

I wiped my tears with the sheet and then dragged my sleeve across my runny nose. "So because a blizzard is coming to Syracuse, we can't go? Can't we stay here for a couple of days and then go? We'd still have plenty of time to get back home."

Daddy shook his head. "It's not just a big snow in Syracuse. There's also a front moving in from the Atlantic. When both air masses collide over Long Island, we're going to be covered in ice."

An ice storm.

I remembered the one from last winter. Schools were closed for four days. Which was why we had to make up those days in June. Which made everybody angry. Which was why I yelled at Jimmy Pulizzi.

But Winter Wonderland was fun while it lasted. Ice glazed everything. Every twig, every telephone wire, every lamp post. When the sun came out, the whole world sparkled. We didn't have electricity for twelve hours, so we wore our coats inside the house and ate peanut butter and jelly sandwiches for dinner.

My hysterics from five minutes ago screeched to a halt and maneuvered a quick U-turn toward gleeful anticipation. "So you're saying we have to get home before the ice storm hits Hampton Shores."

Daddy gave me his "Atta girl" look, like I correctly answered the final question in *Jeopardy*. "Driving in the snow is a piece of cake compared to driving on ice. Not even chains on the tires will be able to grip the road."

I wasn't ready to give up on Francie. "But why can't we stay in Syracuse until after the ice storm, if it happens today?"

Daddy held up two fingers. "One, this storm is supposed to be worse than last year's. Roads may not be navigable for a week or more. Two, I'm due back at the base on Tuesday."

"But you can't help it if the roads close."

"I do know what the weather forecasters are saying, so I should get back to base while I can."

Never let it be said Daddy would shirk his duty. I gave up with a sigh.

How was Francie taking the news? We wouldn't even be able to talk about it on the phone until after I got home. My parents wouldn't let me use Cousin Lynne's phone for an expensive, long-distance call.

Daddy gave me a quick hug, and I breathed in the comforting scent of his aftershave.

Grasping my shoulders, he looked me in the eye. "You ready to come downstairs?"

I hung my head and nodded.

"All right. First thing you do is tell Lynne you're sorry."

I nodded again.

"Then you clean the fry pan. Mom left it in the sink to soak."

Good. I didn't want Mom or anybody else doing that job for me.

Daddy glanced around the room. "I'll strip the sheets and take your suitcase down while you do what I told you."

Chapter 28:
Racing the Storm

Where is my ear-raff?
There. I tuck him close to me.
Time for a long ride.

Cousin Lynne accepted my apology by giving me a big hug. It took almost an hour of scouring with a steel wool pad, but I got that skillet as bright and glossy as if she had bought it yesterday.

Icy air blew into the kitchen from the open door whenever the men and my brothers passed through as they carried luggage to the car. On one of those pass-throughs, Cousin Lynne asked Daddy what kind of magic he'd performed on his daughter.

He grinned at Henry. "Get ready. If you have a boy, he'll copy everything you do. Paul dissected my pipe before he turned two. But if you have a girl? Your little princess will depend on you for everything. Treat her with tender, loving care."

Daddy had dosed me with a lot of TLC earlier, but his words warmed me more than a goose down comforter. I was still his little princess.

In forty-three minutes, the boys and Daddy had all the luggage packed in the car and strapped on the roof. I'd timed them from the kitchen clock while I slaved over that burnt-egg skillet. We piled into the car, Krista included this time. Cousin Lynne gave Mom a sack of goodies for the day. She also placed a book in my hands. *Anne of Green Gables.*

"My *favorite* when I was a kid," she said. "*Enjoy.*"

I admired the cover. A red-haired girl with braids. "Thank you."

She leaned in to give me a final hug. "And don't worry about earlier," she whispered. We can't be perfect all the time."

I decided Lynne was my favorite cousin.

Under the canopy of a metal-gray sky, Dad drove down the long driveway. Paul sat ramrod straight on the hump, and Wade pouted in the cubbyhole. Krista played with her giraffe. How come only the girls were happy? Didn't Daddy tell the boys about the ice storm?

I poked Paul on the shoulder. "You know this is a race, don't you?"

His head jerked around in surprise. "A race?"

Wade leaned over from behind. "A race?"

"Yeah. Daddy told me it's a race. Us against the weather."

The grumpy atmosphere evaporated.

"How do you race the weather?" Wade asked.

Perfect opening. "The snow is going to hit Syracuse and keep heading for New York City, right?"

The boys nodded.

"A second storm is coming up the coast from Florida. And it's going to hit Long Island."

They stared at me, not understanding.

I served up another clue. "The snow is going to meet up with the rain over Hampton Shores."

Paul's eyes gleamed. "The two storms are gonna fight."

"Yup. And when they fight, who's going to win?"

"Snow," they both answered.

"Nope. At first, the rain wins. And the snow melts."

Wade was disgusted. "So it's raining at home? Big deal."

"But then." I slid my eyes to one side trying to look mysterious. "It gets colder. So what happens to the rain?"

"It freezes," Paul said.

I smiled like I was letting them in on a secret. "And what do you get when rain freezes?"

Wade frowned in thought, but Paul shouted his eureka moment. "Ice!"

"And Paul Hansen has won the sixty-four-thousand-dollar question," I announced.

He leaned forward. "Dad. Hampton Shores is getting an ice storm?"

"Looks like it."

Paul continued his thoughts out loud. "A race. We have to stay ahead of the blizzard. Because if the snow beats us, we'll be driving on ice before we make it home."

Daddy lifted one hand off the steering wheel and gave him a thumbs-up.

Paul pounded the back of Daddy's seat. "So, step on it."

I called the first snowflake as we crossed the Throgs Neck Bridge in New York City, and soon thousands of fat flakes swirled around the car. We still had a two-hour drive ahead of us, maybe more. Our unscheduled trip home had put us into the thick of rush-hour. Would traffic jams keep us on the road too long? *Would we lose the race?* Hard to believe these innocent lacy patterns had the potential to ground planes and close highways.

Wade stood on the hump in order to lean over the front seat. "Faster, Dad. The blizzard is catching up with us."

Daddy maintained speed. "We still have a good hour before we need to worry. And by that time, it will probably be all rain."

He turned on the radio. Some kind of classical music with lots of flutes and clarinets rippled through the speakers. "See? They don't have a bunch of storm bulletins going nonstop. The weather service isn't concerned."

By the time we turned into our driveway, the roads were wet, rain had turned to sleet, and the emergency broadcasts beeped a herald of announcements every five minutes.

"An ice storm warning has been issued for all of Long Island, New York City, and north to New Rochelle. Driving will be hazardous. All motorists are advised to stay off the roads after seven o'clock this evening." It was already past seven.

"I don't have enough food in the house if we're stuck here for a couple of days," Mom said. "As soon as we unpack the car, would you run over to the commissary for me?"

Daddy scanned the sky. "We can unpack the car later. Take the kids inside, and I'll be back as soon as I can."

Trying to hurry, Mom fumbled with the strap on Krista's car seat. "I hope they haven't run out of milk with this storm coming."

The commissary, or base grocery store, was maybe five minutes away, but Daddy didn't return for an hour. He arrived with three large sacks filled with milk, bread, fruit, cereal, and fixings for a hamburger dinner. "Sorry it took so long. The place was packed. But they had plenty for everybody."

Since we hadn't stopped for dinner trying to outrace the storm, everyone but Krista was starving. Mom always kept baby food on the cupboard shelves in case regular food was too tough for a little person with only ten teeth.

Mom peered into the bags. "This could do us for an entire week. I hope we won't need all of it."

"Better to be prepared," Daddy said.

The pings of ice on the windowpane seemed to agree with his statement.

We were forced to wait another half hour while Mom made dinner. Listening to hamburger grease spit on the stove and smelling the meat as it fried was torture. And the potato-aroma from the French fries in the oven? Dinner would never taste so good again. We sat at the table and waited.

Mom looked up from flipping the burgers. "Go unpack your suitcases. You might as well get something done while we still have lights to see what we're doing."

That made sense. I had just closed my dresser drawer after laying one last sweater in it when Mom called us back to the kitchen. Stampede for the dinner table.

Paul took a giant bite of his burger. "Can we go outside when we're done eating?"

"Don't talk with your mouth full," Mom automatically responded.

He immediately swallowed, and I was sure I saw a lump of meat slide down his throat the way a snake forces a rat down its gullet.

"Well, can we?"

"Yes, you *may*, as long as you stay in the yard."

We made quick work of the rest of our meal.

Swathed in long johns and snow pants, sweaters and coats, scarves and mittens and boots, we ran out the front door. Ocean air, as cold and wet and salty as a giant mackerel, greeted our exit. Even wearing rubber soles, our feet flew out from underneath us, and we performed a trio of magnificent banana-peel flops landing on our rumps all at the same time. The whole sky sparkled as frozen teardrops fell in front of the streetlights.

Krista stood inside the storm door, her fingers smearing the glass. The look in her eyes told me she longed to join in the fun. What kind of fun would she be allowed to have in that Van Wicked Man place? None.

I slid up the steps and cracked the door open.

"Mom. Let Krista come out, too."

She called back. "Too cold. Too slippery."

"No, really, Mom. She can slide around on her bottom. She'll love it."

After several minutes, Mom set the well-padded, snow-suited Krista on the front step. A scarf was wrapped around her head so only her eyes peeked out from a slit between the layers. I sat down next to her, then pushed off with my mittens and bumped down the steps on my behind. She imitated my motions perfectly and emitted little squeaks with every downward bump. The boys joined us for a few more rounds of "Bump Down the Steps" before we slid across the expanse of the front yard using our boots as ice skates. Krista follow us in a scoot-slide on her knees.

I slowed to a stop by one of the bushes encased in crystal. Krista tried to pull a droplet off one of the bottom branches, but it remained attached. Already, the ice was too thick.

I stuck out my tongue and threw my head back. Tiny bullets of ice shot into my mouth. It almost hurt. Krista copied me, but her little tongue couldn't make it through the layers surrounding her face.

As we performed our own version of ice Olympics, Daddy poked his head out the front door. "Come on in, now. Parts of town have lost power, and I don't like the looks of those electrical lines."

"What's wrong with them?" Wade asked.

We gazed at the sagging, ice-imprisoned wires strung between the telephone poles.

Paul always enjoyed an opportunity to terrify his little brother. "If those things break while we're under 'em, we'll get electrocuted."

"Yeah, I'm going in." Wade backed up, keeping his eyes on the wires until his heel hit the front step, and he almost took another tumble.

We tromped inside leaving a mess of soggy, thawing snow gear on the entryway floor. An hour later, just as I was getting to the most exciting part of my latest book, the lights went out.

Chapter 29:
Bad News

Play "Bump Down the Steps."
Deh-bee, Paw, and Way fall down.
Funny. Makes me laugh.

We woke up to a chilly house and a winter wonderland, its brilliance blinding us in the sunshine. By afternoon, the electricity was back on. The good news—once again, we had a personal ice rink in every front yard and a neighborhood ice rink in the common ground of all of our back yards. We took Krista with us as often as Mom would let us. The bad news—we still had almost a week of Christmas vacation left. We probably wouldn't get one snow day out of this.

Daddy dropped his bombshell when we sat down to dinner on New Year's Day. "We were able to get an appointment for Krista at St. Alban's on January twelfth. We're going to figure out once and for all why she doesn't talk and walk properly."

St. Alban's? The gray military hospital? How

could they send her back to that awful place exactly one year after she was tortured there?

"Have they painted the walls yet?" I asked, knowing full well that would never happen.

Daddy stared at me for a moment, his eyes bleak with sympathy. He understood.

Mom didn't. "If we can find out what's going on with her, then it's worth the gray walls."

"Why can't she go to Southampton's hospital instead?"

Daddy's voice was gentle "They're not equipped for it, Debbie."

"How long does she have to stay in the hospital?" Wade asked.

Yeah, he remembered how bad it was last year.

"Two to three weeks. They'll check ears, eyes, heart, muscles, spine, everything."

I remembered a baby who never stopped crying. "Two to three weeks? You're going to put her through—"

"Deborah Lynne!" Mom's voice, sharp and deadly, stopped me from uttering the cuss word she knew was coming. "When you're an adult, you'll understand that putting a child through temporary misery can bring blessings in the long run. *That's* what we're doing."

I glanced around the table. Wade was crying. Paul mechanically shoveled spoonful after spoonful of mashed potatoes into his mouth. He never said much when feelings ran high, and I couldn't read his face or eyes either. Oblivious to the drama surrounding her, Krista was busy trying to stab a piece of pork chop with her baby fork.

I lifted my chin in sullen defiance. "May I be

excused? I'm not hungry."

"No." Daddy tried to stroke my arm, but I pulled away. "Debbie, remember how you've always thought Krista is deaf?"

I nodded, staring at my plate.

"Your mother and I agree with you." My head jerked up to meet his eyes, his gaze broadcasting reassurance. "But the only way to find out for sure is to do some tests."

"You don't need a hospital to test somebody's ears. We have hearing tests at school."

"True." He reached for my hand, and this time I allowed it. "But we have to do a check on her heart every year, and with everything else we want investigated, a hospital stay is in order. Once we have the answers to our questions, Krista shouldn't need to go to the hospital for a long time."

"Promise?"

"I can never promise the future." He squeezed my hand. "But the way things are right now, I wouldn't expect any long hospital visits."

I still wanted to leave the dinner table. I needed a good cry. But Daddy wasn't done with bad news.

"There's something else the three of you need to know."

That would be me, Paul and Wade.

Mom suddenly found the napkin in her lap very interesting. Wade looked terrified. How much worse could things get?

Daddy continued. "You've heard Mom and me discuss world news like the war in Vietnam?"

Paul shoved his half-full plate to the center of the table. My lips remained closed, but my mind was screaming. *No, no, no, no, no!* Wade frowned at Paul's reaction. He didn't understand yet. Krista was now licking potatoes off of her fingers instead of using her spoon.

Daddy took a deep breath. "Well, fighter pilots get assigned to Vietnam for a year. This summer, it will be my turn."

Everything that was important five minutes ago turned into meaningless trash like confetti after a parade. Wishing Chip would kiss me? Way down on the list. Sarah leaving? We'd both survived before. Missing Francie? Dad had promised we'd go back in February—weather permitting. Krista in the hospital? She just dropped a notch from the number one position of worries.

Daddy fighting in a war. That was *big.*

Paul walked away from the table without asking for permission. I couldn't take the stricken look on Wade's face as Daddy's words sank in. I ran to my room.

Throwing myself on the bed left me too exposed. Where could I curl up and hide? In a house filled with six people, privacy barely existed. I couldn't walk outside and wander the neighborhood in the dark in the middle of winter. But I refused to give in to tears until I found a space where no one would bother me.

The closet. It wasn't large, but I crawled in, pushing shoes and forgotten books and clothes toward the entrance while creating a space in the back corner. How ironic. I usually stuffed worries in the back corner of the closet of my mind. Now, I was stuffing *myself* into a real closet.

I knelt in the dark, resting my forehead on the floor

and using the chest of my old, abandoned teddy bear as a pillow. Then I sobbed without sound, so no one would hear. I didn't want comfort. There was no comfort tonight.

Someone stepped into the room. "Debbie?" Daddy spoke in a low voice.

"I want to be alone."

"Okay." He stepped back into the hall.

Was this how Jimmy Pulizzi felt? Had he known his dad was going to Vietnam that day I yelled at him on the bus? The thought of causing him more pain added to mine. Now, like him, I would be wondering if my mom would get a phone call, or if solemn men would knock on our door with the worst news. That happened to Mom's friend around the block. The officers' wives took turns sitting with the lady and taking care of her kids until she moved away to restart life in the civilian world.

Every terrifying possibility shooting into my mind brought on another bout of tremors and tears. They soaked into my cotton-stuffed friend.

What was life going to be like without Daddy? Mom would need my help. When Daddy had been assigned to Alaska for a year, she had depended on me to keep my toddler brothers out of trouble, to entertain them when she was busy doing the work of both a father and a mother.

I didn't want to face that kind of responsibility. Just let me stay huddled in the closet, a miserable, damp mess.

At some point Daddy's footsteps returned. I heard him settle himself on the floor on the other side of the closet door. He gently tapped on it. "Debbie?"

"What?"

"Mom needs to put Krista to bed."

I didn't move.

"Do you remember when Mom told you the problems we expected with Krista?"

A muffled "yes" whispered out of me. I had worried about what would happen with a not normal baby. I hadn't even met her yet. I couldn't picture life where someone in the family was blind or deaf or crippled.

"And have there been problems?"

"Yes."

"Have those problems made our lives miserable?"

"No."

Except for hospitals, life had been great. Krista was the best little sister a kid could have.

"Krista *has* been a blessing, hasn't she?"

"Yeah, but that's not the same as going to war. What if we never see you again?"

Daddy was silent a moment. "Actually, we might not have ever seen Krista again after her heart operation. So in a way, they *are* the same."

My head jerked up. So Francie had been *right* last summer? And my parents never let on? Other than talking about how the surgery involved cutting her almost in half, they had never referred to how risky that time had been.

I choked out, "But Krista *didn't* die."

"No, she didn't, and I give both the doctors and God the credit for that."

I slid into an upright kneeling position and clutched the teddy bear to my chest. All my prayers had been answered with a *yes*—that I would get a sister, that Krista would be born alive, that if anything had to be wrong, it would be deafness. The doctors might disagree on that last one, but I was pretty sure God was giving me the nod.

"I'm asking you to trust God for the time I'm in Vietnam. Can you do that?"

I didn't know. The girl who had fully expected God to give her a sister wasn't so sure of the future anymore. "What if you d—What if you never come home?"

"Then I'm asking you to trust God with that sadness, too."

Would I even be able *live* with that kind of sorrow?

But I couldn't bear to disappoint him. "I'll try."

He stood and opened the door. "Where are you? Have I been talking to the Invisible Girl?" All he could see was the pile of stuff on the floor

He could always force a giggle out of me. I stretched out a leg, now tingling with pins and needles. Scooting gingerly, I allowed him to help me out of the closet, and then he wrapped me in a long, long hug.

Except for Alaska, he'd always been nearby with those hugs every day. *And* for every special event. My first piano recital. All of my birthdays. Even when I broke our kitchen window. Who knew I had the ability to send a pebble flying that distance the first time I tried out a slingshot? Despite his anger, Daddy had hugged me and wiped my tears until I was reassured of his forgiveness.

"Ready?" He released his hold and peered into my eyes. I could see into his soul. Peace. Love. Strength.

Maybe those things resided in my soul, too. After all, I was Grant Hansen's daughter.

"Yes." My words came out a bit shaky.

He kept his hand on my shoulder as we walked out of my room to face 1967.

Chapter 30:
A Soldier's Fears

I was here before.
The gray place. The hurting place.
I want to go home.

O n January twelfth, they took Krista away to the gray chamber of horrors. That's how the boys and I still felt about it, like an evil army had captured her and thrown her in a dungeon. Except Mom and Daddy were the evil soldiers, and the hospital room was Krista's prison cell.

I had thought about teaching her signs for hospital and doctor and nurse but figured she still wouldn't understand. No toddler would. She probably didn't even remember her last hospital stay. I was wrong.

The first night, Mom ended up staying there because Krista wouldn't stop crying. They hadn't even started the tests yet, but she *knew* the place was scary and dangerous.

Just like when Krista had her heart surgery, Paul and Wade fought over every little thing, and I cried over stuff as ridiculous as the toothpaste cap rolling off the counter. Mom and Daddy didn't talk about what happened each day in the hospital, which left me in the dark, which was worse than knowing the worst, which brought on nightmares about tortured children in the pediatric ward. Tales from the Zombie Hospital.

Each dream was almost the same. Gray doctors and nurses wandered the hallways with grim faces. They didn't eat the patients, but they ignored them. One night, I dreamed they walked past wailing babies lying on the floor. Another night, they stood around an operating table and stared at the sleeping patient. Then they walked away.

I woke up every morning totally depressed. I was living in a never-ending episode of *The Twilight Zone*.

At least, school kept me busy, and I made sure to find reasons to take the late bus home every day. I stayed for choir practice two afternoons a week. On the other days, I sat in the bleachers and did my homework while the seventh-grade basketball team practiced. Any home games were also after school, so along with Melissa and Leigh and a bunch of other girls in our group, I watched Chip and the rest of the team.

When I got home on the seventh day of Krista's imprisonment, Daddy was at the stove stirring tomato soup. He had grilled cheese sandwiches browning in the skillet. I wanted to gag. Why couldn't we have steaks? Grilling those was his specialty.

Daddy grabbed a metal spatula to flip the sandwiches. "The boys are next door. Run over and tell them dinner's about ready." He didn't even look up to say hi.

"Where's Mom?"

She usually tried to leave the hospital in the

afternoon to get home to cook dinner.

"She's going to stay there."

My heart thudded into my stomach. "What happened?"

"Go get your brothers." He kept his back turned and *ignored* me. My zombie nightmares were coming true.

Five minutes later, the boys and I sat at the kitchen table, bowls of soup steaming in front of us, each with our own plate of grilled cheese. I crumbled at least six saltine crackers into my soup to make it edible, but it didn't help the sickening smell.

Daddy had made nothing for himself. He left the kitchen once he served the food.

Paul chowed down his sandwich while the soup cooled. Wade slurped a spoonful and yelped. He ran to the freezer for an ice cube.

Paul laughed. "You do that all the time. Why don't you put the ice cube in the soup to begin with?"

And that was all it took to start Round 271 of this week's Paul-Wade slugfest. Instead of dropping the ice cube into his bowl, Wade fired it, hitting Paul right between the eyes. Paul slammed against the table as he jumped up and grabbed the ice cube tray from Wade, sending soup sloshing onto the table from everyone's bowls.

"Aw, c'mon." I sopped up soup around my bowl with a paper napkin. "Cut it out, guys."

They didn't listen.

Paul put pressure on the tray to loosen all the ice, then snapped it forward like he was launching a rubber band. "I think you need to cool down, Squirt."

Flying cubes hit Wade in the chest, then created a

rat-a-tat-tat on the floor. Some sailed past him smacking the opposite wall, and a couple landed on the table. One sat on my sandwich, already melting. Daddy wouldn't make me choke down a *soggy* grilled cheese, would he?

Wade snatched back the metal tray and tried to beat Paul with it. "You think you're so cool. How about an ice helmet?"

His efforts were futile. Paul had shot up a few inches this fall while Wade was still short and scrawny. With an evil smirk, Paul used one arm to hold Wade at bay and the other to shove the tray toward Wade's chin.

"*Enough!*" Dad's bellow echoed through the house and possibly up the chimney.

The ice tray clanged to the floor, then silence.

We'd never received more than measured spankings for outright disobedience, but when Daddy got angry, the ferocious look on his face terrified us.

"You two." He glared at the boys. "Get in your pajamas and go to bed. I don't want to hear a *whisper* from your room the rest of the night."

I glanced at the clock on the stove. Not quite six. Paul and Wade didn't argue. They shuffled out, Paul in the lead. Wade turned back to send a look of longing toward his soup bowl before following.

Daddy's glare turned on me. What did *I* do?

"Clean up this mess."

"But I—"

His jaw tensed, and his eyes tightened to blue slits.

Too shocked to cry, I gathered the plates of sandwiches with no further protest and gently moved them to the sink. After the bedlam of the last few minutes, I didn't want to hear one more sharp noise.

Should I throw all the food away? *Someone* might want their sandwich warmed in the oven tomorrow. Daddy had already disappeared from the kitchen, so it was my call.

I poured soup down the sink and wrapped up the sandwiches except for my soggy one. I mopped up the mess on the table and whatever had dribbled off the edge. After I wiped the ice water dripping down the wall, I started on the floor.

Mini-puddles with a sliver of ice in their centers dotted the tiles. Snagging a thin slice of ice was a lot trickier than plucking up a large cube. Each sliver swam away from me more than once. I had to chase them across the kitchen, creating more melt-off with each attempt. As for the one that slid under the stove, it was just going to have evaporate under there.

This was what my life had been like for the past year or more. Chasing after slippery clues as to what was wrong with Krista. The only solid cube we'd been able to pick up and deal with was the hole in her heart. One major surgery and done. But trying to figure out why she didn't walk yet, why she didn't talk at all? We'd been skidding all over Long Island, sliding into walls of doctors who didn't care. But unlike the ice water under the stove, we couldn't just abandon Krista in some institution like the doctors wanted. We needed to clean up every icy puddle that messed up her life.

I moved from one chore to the next, kind of mindless…like a zombie. I didn't want to think about our problems anymore. Not about ice, not about the hospital. After retrieving the last ice sliver, I used rags to dry the floor. Then, I washed and dried the dishes and put them away in the cabinets.

In all that time, the house was completely silent. No television or radio. No voices at all. I'd probably have nightmares about my zombie *house*. Except, weren't zombies dead people walking? Maybe Paul, Wade, and I were so much alive that Krista's stay in the hospital hurt too much, and since we didn't know what to do about it, we did everything wrong.

The clean kitchen rivaled Mom's handiwork as I hung the damp dishcloth over the oven's broad handle. Daddy entered, retrieved a glass from the cupboard, and filled it with milk. After all that work and no dinner, milk looked good to me, too. Daddy noticed my eyes on his glass. He handed it to me, then returned to the cupboard for another.

Should I sit down or take my milk to the living room and get out of his way? Did I dare ask a question?

He guzzled down the milk and poured a second glass. Then he set it on the table, pulled out a chair for himself, and sat down with a loud exhale. I took a seat across from him and sipped my milk. So much better than tomato soup.

"Daddy?" My voice sounded so small I might as well have been three years old again.

He looked at me. His face wasn't ferocious anymore, just bone-weary.

"Will you tell me what's going on? Why Mom had to stay at the hospital?"

"Krista needed Mom more than usual tonight, that's all." His non-answer did *not* ease my fears. "Debbie, if you're worried that Krista is dying, don't. She's fine."

"I'm not worried that she's going to die. I'm worried she might be in pain, but I don't know if she is or she isn't, which makes things even worse."

He still didn't give me a direct answer. "Of course, she's not comfortable. Most people have to go through uncomfortable procedures in a hospital."

If Krista wasn't dying, then why wasn't he telling me the truth? How bad could it be?

"Daddy?"

"Hmmm?"

"Remember when you let me go to the hospital with you after Krista's heart operation?"

"You cried."

"I know. Do you remember what I said?"

He tilted his head in thought. "Not exactly. Other than you hated the gray walls."

"I said I'd rather feel scared and know what I was afraid of than feel more scared and *not* know what I was afraid of."

He nodded.

"And back then, when I saw Krista so tiny and sad, I cried. But because I knew what she was going through, because I knew about her sadness, somehow, I could face the whole situation without feeling so afraid. I don't know why."

A hint of a smile touched his lips, and a small light flickered in his eyes, chasing away the exhaustion. "I know why."

I blinked. He did?

"Soldiers feel the same way sometimes. Before a battle, they need some facts. If they know their enemy and where it's hiding, they can figure out a strategy to defeat it. But if they don't know who the enemy is or where something might jump out at them, they can never relax. Their only plan is to be on the defense.

And you can't win a war that way."

"I'm not in a war."

"Not exactly a war. But you—all of us—are in a battle to help Krista overcome whatever's wrong. Until we know what's wrong, we can't figure out a strategy to help her. So consider this hospital stay a scouting mission. We'll learn more so we can plan victory." He leaned over and kissed my forehead. "In your case, not knowing what's happening with Krista, even while we search for answers, makes you feel like the soldier who doesn't know where the enemy is. You can't begin to devise a strategy to help your sister."

His words made sense, which helped me push home my point. "So are you going to let me know why Mom had to stay at the hospital?"

A sound that was half sigh and half "harrumph" came out of him. "Maybe I should."

"Will you tell me, too?" Paul stood at the door to the front hall. Out of bed against orders, he shifted his feet ready to fly back to his room at Daddy's first growl.

Chapter 31:
Waiting

Big pain. Where's Mah-mi?
Big scary. My hands can't move.
I cry, "Ma. Ma. Ma."

Daddy considered Paul's request while staring at my brother's bare feet. "Get some slippers and tell Wade I don't want *him* out of bed."

Paul returned in seconds. "Wade fell asleep."

"Good."

Daddy motioned him forward. My brother stood stiff and straight like a soldier waiting to be dressed down by his commanding officer for bad behavior, except Paul was in blue-checked pajamas.

"You have a history of making your brother miserable when you're angry with him—or the rest of the world."

Paul's eyes met Daddy's without flinching.

"I think you're old enough to know what's going on with your little sister, but Wade is not." He paused to let those words sink in. Paul didn't move a muscle.

"And the next time Wade makes you mad, are you going to tell him what I'm about to tell you, just to make him miserable?"

"No."

Daddy gave him a hard stare.

"I promise." Paul crossed his heart, then offered his Boy Scout salute.

Daddy patted the chair beside him, and Paul moved to it.

But Daddy's words had terrified me. If Wade couldn't handle Krista's problems, would I be able to? Had I meant what I said? *Was* it better for me to know bad news than to know nothing?

Again, I thought back to Krista's heart surgery, and I had the answer to my question. Ignorance was *not* bliss.

"Okay." Daddy took a deep breath. "This whole first week, they've done tests for Krista's ears and eyes, they've poked and prodded her legs and arms. Nothing real painful, but of course, like you guys would be, she's scared. She doesn't know why people are doing this to her. I think the only reason Mom can come home at all is because Krista knows she'll be back in the morning, and the afternoon nurse showers her with treats and cuddles."

He gave me a pointed look as if to say, *See, not all the doctors and nurses are grim.*

"Today was the big day, the toughest test." He paused, looked Paul and me in the eye, signaling for us to get ready. "They needed to test her brain and nervous system, so they performed a spinal tap. Do you know what that is?"

Paul shook his head. I was still thinking.

A *spinal tap.* I pictured a doctor with a hammer tapping lightly up and down someone's backbone.

Daddy told me differently. "They slide a very large needle in between the little bones that make up your backbone and remove some of the fluid that's in between. Then they do tests with the fluid to find out if anything's wrong in the brain."

A large needle? In the bony part of your back? *Owwww.* I felt sick.

Paul asked, "Like what the Indians used to tap maple trees? They stuck a tube in the trunk and took out the sap?"

Obviously, he was only interested in the mechanics, he hadn't considered how that might feel to Krista. Then his eyes got big. "They tapped Krista like a maple tree?"

Daddy squeezed his hand. "The needle wasn't *that* big. And when the doctor does it right, it doesn't hurt more than a shot."

A lump formed in my throat. "Did they do it right?"

"Yes, but the hardest part comes after they take out the fluid. Since all that liquid got jostled around, Krista has to lie on her back for a whole day. If she moves much or sits up, the fluid won't settle back to where it originally was, and she'll get a terrible headache."

The pulse in my head started to thump just thinking about it. "Did Mom have to stay because Krista has a headache?"

"We're not sure. She cries and cries. But we don't know if it's because she's strapped to the cradle board to keep her still, or if she has a headache from the procedure."

"She definitely has a headache," I said. "If I cry for a long time, I get a headache. So whether it's the spinal tap or the crying, her head is hurting." My poor baby sister.

"How long does the headache last?" Paul asked.

"If it comes from the spinal tap, it may last a couple days." He sighed. "Baby aspirin will help, but if she's crying because she's scared and tired?" He shook his head. "I don't know what could help."

Krista cried most of Thursday, too, but by Friday, she was allowed to move around, and that made her happier.

Mom came home every night and let us know what kinds of tests Krista was given each day. Some days they let her play with toys, and they wrote down what she did with them. Psychological tests, Mom explained. Nothing else the doctors did came close to the pain of the spinal tap. They expected to be finished by Tuesday, and they'd send her home.

My gray, zombie hospital nightmares stopped. Instead, silly dream fragments created a slide show in my brain. Click. Angel nurses fluttered around Krista's crib. Click. Doctors danced a soft-shoe entrance into Krista's room, holding giant hypodermic needles. When they pointed at the baby, the needles popped open like umbrellas, except the umbrellas were lollipops. Click. A greyhound harnessed to a little red wagon pulled Krista through the hospital corridors. She was laughing. And all those dream snapshots were in bright colors like the Land of the Munchkins from the *Wizard of Oz*.

On Tuesday afternoon, I took the early bus and skipped choir practice, but no one was home when I got there. I ran next door to see if Mrs. Gaston had heard anything. She reassured me that hospitals are often slow to release patients, and if she heard from my parents, she'd let me know. I should've stayed for choir.

The boys arrived home at the same time the phone rang. I raced to answer it.

"Debbie?" Mom's voice sounded distant.

"Mom! Are you still at the hospital?"

"Yes. We have an extra meeting with the staff to discuss test results. This way, we don't have to return next week."

"You mean they already know what's wrong with Krista?"

She kept talking like she didn't hear my question. "We're not going to get home for at least another three hours. Probably more with city traffic. Do you think you could make some supper for you and the boys?"

"Sure." I'd never cooked in my life, but I'd watched Mom plenty of times.

Her tinny voice continued. "There's canned soup in the cabinet and plenty of bread and lunchmeat for sandwiches."

I was so sick of soup and sandwiches. I had to figure out something better.

"If you have trouble, call Mrs. Gaston, okay? I need to go. Tell the boys to be good."

"Wait. What did you find out? Mom?" I was talking to a dead phone.

Paul stood at the entrance to the kitchen.

Wade's feet pounded down the back hall. "Mom! Where's Krista?"

Paul regarded the phone in my hand. "That was Mom?"

"Yeah. They haven't left yet."

His body stiffened into an alert stance ready to defend against bad news. "What went wrong?"

I hung up the phone. "Nothing. The doctors decided to give them some of the test results today so it's taking longer than they thought."

He relaxed. "Good. I didn't want to wait."

I nodded. We both wanted answers. Now.

"Where's Mom and Dad? Where's Krista?" Wade skidded to a stop from his race back to the kitchen.

"They'll get home sometime after dinner." I pointed to the coats they dropped in the front hall. "Will you guys please hang those up in the closet?"

As they moved to do so, Paul said, "So what are we supposed to do for dinner? Go next door?"

"I'm cooking."

He snorted. "Soup and peanut butter and jelly, right?"

I ignored his assumptions. "I think I could make us spaghetti."

Paul snorted again, but Wade practically drooled. "I love spaghetti. You really think you can make it?"

"How hard can it be? Mom boils it in one pot and heats the sauce in another pot."

"Do we have garlic bread?" Paul asked.

I checked the bread drawer. "No. But maybe I can butter regular bread and put some garlic powder on it."

He looked doubtful. "And are you gonna make salad, too?"

Hmm. That might be tricky slicing up cucumbers and tomatoes. Sharp knives made me nervous. "I can try.”

“We can help.”

I stared at Wade. He didn’t spill things like he used to, but …

“Okay.” I took a moment to figure out my strategy. “Wade, you fill the big pot with water. Paul, you get the spaghetti, sauce, and can opener, and a small pot. I’ll see what’s in the refrigerator for salad, and I’ll butter the bread.”

With only a little spillover, Wade maneuvered the pot out from under the faucet and transferred it to the stove. He turned the large burner on *high*. Paul had no trouble getting the sauce out of the can and into a smaller pot. He set it on a small burner and turned it on *high*. I gathered vegetables from the refrigerator, a knife from the drawer, and the wooden cutting board.

Wade watched me tear the lettuce and place the pieces in three little bowls. “Doesn’t Mom wash that?”

“Don’t be ridiculous. Who wants soap on their lettuce?” I continued to place several leaves in each bowl.

His brow wrinkled. “I know I’ve seen her put it all on paper towels to dry.”

“Well, I’m not doing that tonight.”

I smelled something burning. The sauce. It was spitting red blobs all over the stove. I rushed over and pulled the pot off the burner so it would stop bubbling. Stirring it with a large spoon, I could tell stuff was stuck to the bottom. Paul grabbed the spoon from me and started scraping.

I tried to stop his hand. “No. Leave it. It’s already burnt down there.”

Too late. Black bits floated to the top.

"Oh." He studied the results of his vigorous work with the spoon. After he set the pot on the counter, remembering to place a potholder underneath it, he pulled a teaspoon from the drawer and began lifting the black flakes out of the pot and into the sink.

"Good thinking." I watched his painstaking attention to detail. He targeted every little black speck. "Wow."

He looked up from his work. "What?"

"If this had happened while Mom was here, we'd be screaming at each other by now."

His concentration returned to the pot. "Nobody here but us to clean up the mess. Yelling wouldn't get it done."

Another amazing change—Wade wasn't on the verge of panic. Maybe he was confident Paul and I would get in trouble over burnt pots and dirty lettuce since none of it was his fault.

"What else do you want me to do?" he asked.

Then again, maybe he just wanted to be part of the team.

"You can set the table." I pointed to the silverware drawer and returned to my salad.

Time to pare and slice the cucumber. I cut off the ends, two satisfying thuds as the knife sliced to the board. Then I cut it into small chunks. Paul glanced up in time to see me pare the skin ever...so...carefully...around one of the chunks, taking almost half the cucumber with it.

"We won't have any cucumber to eat if you do that all the way around it."

"I don't want to cut myself."

"You want me to do it?"

Maybe I should have stayed in Girl Scouts to learn some practical skills. Paul was a Tenderfoot Boy Scout this year, and he knew all kinds of survival stuff.

I set down the knife, and we switched places. He expertly skinned ribbons of cucumber peel while I concentrated on picking out burned dots of sauce.

"Watch out!" Wade's sudden shout caused me to jump back from the counter.

With a whoosh, boiling water foamed over the big pot. I grabbed two towels, lifted the pot, and placed it on an unused burner. Who knew spaghetti was so complicated?

The three of us stared at our workspace. The stove had a small, hot lake on it, but at least the water immediately dissolved the splats of red sauce. The lettuce I didn't use sat on the counter looking like a dissected volleyball. Cucumber peels formed a fringe around the cutting board. The tomato sat in pristine beauty. For the moment.

"What do we do now?" Wade asked.

I turned both knobs on the stove to *off*. "Let's soak up the water with more dish towels." I moved to the correct drawer for those. "Paul, could you slice up the tomato, too? And don't put any in my bowl." Tomatoes were pretty but tasted terrible.

He turned back to the cutting board.

"Wade, get out the bread. And butter six slices."

The rest of our preparations didn't go too badly. I turned on the oven for the bread, and the burners went back on, *low* for the sauce and *medium* for the spaghetti water, which I watched over carefully. Wade put the slices on the broiler pan. They had a few holes in them due to the fact that it's hard to spread cold margarine on soft bread. I stuck the tray in the oven. The slices toasted perfectly, not one blackened crust.

There was one tricky moment when I couldn't figure out how to get the spaghetti out of the pot but then remembered Mom poured it all into a colander in the sink. The two-minute delay in finding the colander left the spaghetti a little overcooked and mushy.

The whole meal was ready before five o'clock. I never realized you could make a dinner in less than an hour, but eating early allowed us more time to clean up. And boy, that was going to take a long time.

Three plates of spaghetti sat at our places. Salad bowls on the left. Glasses of milk on the right. A platter piled with bread filled the center. A table worthy of admiration.

We sat down to our very own spaghetti dinner. We couldn't even taste the few black flakes that were left in the sauce. The tomatoes in the boys' salads appeared to be smashed—apparently tomatoes were harder to slice than cucumbers—but Paul and Wade seemed happy to eat them. And our garlic bread? Yum! Wade had been extra generous with the garlic powder. When Mom and Daddy got home, they would keel over as soon as we breathed on them.

We'd better brush our teeth before kissing Krista.

Chapter 32:
Diagnosis

I smell puh-eddy.
Yum! Deh-bee sees me and cries.
Don't worry. I'm fine!

After-dinner cartoons played on the TV when Mom, Daddy, and Krista stepped into our house. The plates were washed, the blackened pot still soaked in soapy water, and the counter had been scrubbed of all tomato body parts. As soon as she saw her brothers and sister, a pale Krista, clutching a small, pink, heart-shaped pillow, leaned out of Daddy's arms for one of us to hold her. Paul heaved her onto his shoulder, and Wade and I were almost in tears as we smothered her with hugs and kisses and freshly mouth-washed breaths.

Mom sniffed the garlicky air and scanned the kitchen. Her gaze landed on the colander drying on the drain board. "Debbie. You made spaghetti?"

"Yes."

But Wade wouldn't let me have all the glory. "Paul

and I helped, too."

She gave him a squeeze. "And what did *you* do?"

Of course, he told her every detail. She oohed and aahed, but I didn't care about that. I wanted answers.

"What did you learn about the tests?"

She shrugged off her coat. "Give us a moment to get settled, okay? And we haven't had any dinner yet."

With a proud smile, Paul pointed to the fridge "There's leftovers in the refrigerator."

While Mom and Daddy hung up coats and made trips to the bathroom, I dumped the spaghetti back into a clean pot and reheated it all, on *low*. I buttered and garlicked more bread and put it in the still-warm oven. But I wasn't making another salad.

Wade set the table. Paul pulled out three more plates and two glasses from the cupboards. While I loaded each plate with spaghetti and sauce, Paul poured water into the glasses.

Mom returned with Krista, who still held onto her pink pillow.

"Can I see?" I asked, pointing to my chest, then my eye, then the pillow.

Mom didn't do her usual lips-pressed-together thing when she saw me signing. Maybe she was so glad to have Krista home, she didn't care about anything else.

Krista handed it over. The expression in her eyes told me I'd better treat it kindly.

It was a satin heart with 2 googly eyes sewed on to it as well as a big, cross-stitched smile. I caressed my face with it. "Soft." I needed to look up the sign for *soft*.

Krista reached for it and copied my motion.

"The staff gave that to her as a going away present," Mom said.

Maybe the hospital wasn't as gray and hopeless as I'd thought.

Mom popped Krista into her highchair, then took her own seat. "My, this is great service."

She tied a bib around Krista's neck and insisted on removing the heart from the chair's tray. Krista's frown cleared up when I set her plate of spaghetti in its place. Paul served Daddy, and Wade, wearing clumsy oven mitts, concentrated on *not* dropping the hot plate of bread. My parents looked at each other, and a secret smile passed between them, something that happened a lot in our house.

After allowing them their first bite of food, the boys and I couldn't stand it any longer.

"What did you find out?"

"What did the tests say?"

"What things are wrong with Krista?"

We all spoke at once.

Daddy set down his fork. Fear tried to bludgeon my hopes until his first words gave me temporary relief. "Let's begin with the good news. The doctors were wrong. Krista is *not* mentally retarded. She will not have trouble learning. She will not regress back to babyhood."

Krista looked up from her plate of spaghetti and watched the clapping and cheers. With a grin, she waved her spoon in the air to join in.

"And there's nothing wrong with her overall health." Mom removed the spoon from Krista's sauce-covered fingers and laid it on her plate. "No diabetes, her heart is fine, nothing to stop her from growing."

I knew there was more. "But…"

Daddy offered a sad smile. "There are three major issues. All of them can be overcome or dealt with, but it will take time."

If it could be dealt with, I could handle it. When a soldier knows his enemy, he can make a strategy to defeat it.

Daddy took another bite of spaghetti before continuing. "First, Krista's eyes. The left one is fine. The right one with the cataract? The one that rolls in toward her nose?" We nodded in understanding. "They can fix it so she's not cross-eyed, but she she'll only see light and blurred motions. Glasses won't make it any better."

Okay, God. Thank you that she's not blind. But she's only got one eye left. Please take care of it.

Mom directed Paul to retrieve her purse from the front hall closet. With the crackle of paper, she pulled out some crumpled pages and placed them on the table.

"Then they found out why she can't walk." She smoothed the papers as she spoke. "The muscles in her legs are called *spastic*. They're too tight. They don't stretch. It's a form of cerebral palsy."

Daddy squeezed Mom's hand, and she rested her cheek against their intertwined fingers. "So she stands on tiptoe because that's more comfortable for her than on a flat foot."

I pointed my toes, then flexed my foot several times. The muscles in my calf stretched whenever I flexed. Krista couldn't do that.

Mom pointed to one of the papers. "But doctors can help those muscles stretch. We have exercises we can do at home with her."

The boys and I leaned forward and studied the diagrams. They looked pretty simple.

"Plus, we go back in a couple weeks and fit her for leg braces."

"She has to go back to the hospital?" Wade wailed out loud. I was doing the same inside.

"No, no. She doesn't have to stay." Mom held up a glossy brochure showing a kid wearing long metal bars down his legs with straps tying the bars together. "Doctors have already done the measurements, and in two weeks the braces should be ready. Therapists want to make sure they fit, and we'll practice putting them on."

I watched Krista use her fingers to lift cut pieces of spaghetti from her plate to her spoon. She was *not* going to like another trip to the hospital.

"How do the braces work?" Paul tilted his head as he studied the boy in the brochure.

Daddy replied, "I'm not sure of the technical details, but the idea is that while she wears them, they're stretching those muscles a tiny bit all the time."

"Will it hurt?" Wade's big blue eyes pooled with tears before he even heard the answer.

Daddy patted his hand. "No. They don't hurt."

"How long does she have to wear them?" I had needed crutches for three weeks after I pulled ligaments in my foot during ballet class. I figured Krista would need braces for longer than that.

Mom answered with another question. "How long during the day, or how long will she need to wear them before they do their job of stretching the muscles enough?

"I was wondering how many weeks it will take, but

I guess how many hours each day is important to know, too."

"We're not measuring weeks, Debbie." Daddy's next words slid into a sigh. "It'll take years. As Krista grows, the muscles need to keep stretching."

Years.

Krista noticed the brochure and grabbed it from Mom, peering at the picture of the happy little boy wearing leg braces. She bent to peek under her tray, straightened up again, and beamed at me as she patted her own leg. I tried to smile back, but my lips didn't want to move in that direction.

"And she'll wear them every day, all day. It will be like putting on her clothes." Mom tried to make it sound easy, but her nervous smile exposed the lie.

Poor Krista. And that was only problem number two. I assumed problem number three was even more serious.

Paul posed my question. "What about the third thing?"

"Ah." Daddy rubbed the back of his neck. He looked straight at me. "Debbie was right all along. Krista can't hear."

"So the doctors admitted they've been wrong?" I had a hard time picturing Dr. Winkler admitting to being anything less than perfect. But then, he wasn't one of the hospital doctors.

"They explained they'd misjudged things because Krista could neither walk nor talk. The combination of cerebral palsy and deafness made it *look* like she was cognitively slow." He kept his gaze on me. "Doctors are kind of like detectives in your mystery books. Sometimes, the clues lead to a dead end."

Why did his words make me feel guilty? The doctors were wrong, and I had been *right*.

Daddy continued with the detective comparison. "But now we know the culprits and what to do with them." His eyes hadn't stopped boring into me. "Are you ready to get off your high horse and cooperate with the doctors now that they're sure of how to help Krista?"

That last thought that *the doctors were wrong and I was right* did sound arrogant. I'd been so eager to be proved right, I'd forgotten what was most important. Would I rather keep hating the doctors for *their* arrogance, or would I prefer to work with them?

I had to drop my gaze so Daddy couldn't see into my soul. Debbie, the *nice* girl, Debbie the *sweet* girl, had *hated* a group of people who were trying to help a baby.

The doctors weren't perfect. And neither was I.

Soldier Debbie slipped off her high horse and responded to Daddy's question. "Yes, sir. As long as they don't want to send her to an institution, I'll do whatever they say."

I knew my enemy now, and it wasn't the doctors. If they had a plan to defeat cerebral palsy and deafness, I would join them and do my part.

Until now, we had played with sign language, but I hadn't thought about what it *meant* to be deaf. The beginning of understanding rolled over me like an avalanche down a mountainside.

Krista. Couldn't. Hear.

She had never heard my voice. She'd never heard *any* voices. She'd never heard a dog bark or a bird sing or rain patter on the roof. I listened in the silence following Daddy's words. The clock ticked on the wall. The refrigerator hummed. The furnace thumped on, and the heated air whispered gently through the vents. Krista had no idea any of those sounds existed.

Paul was ready to fix whatever was broken. "What will the doctors do so she can hear?"

Daddy hesitated before he answered. "She'll wear hearing aids."

Paul frowned. "Like the horns old people stick in their ears?"

The same picture from an old Mickey Mouse cartoon crossed my mind, too.

If the situation weren't so serious, Daddy would've laughed. "It looks like a small walkie-talkie, and it has wires connected to it with earplug-like things on the other end. We put the ear plugs in her ears, turn on the hearing aids, and they make everything around her louder, so she can hear."

"Like a radio?" Wade asked. "She'll be able to turn a knob and make it louder or softer?"

"Exactly. She can control the volume."

"Does she have to wear hearing aids for years, too?" I didn't even like to use ear plugs in the pool. Too uncomfortable.

Daddy hesitated again. "For the rest of her life, Debbie."

A second avalanche piled over the first. "She will never be able to hear without hearing aids." Tears threatened.

Krista had moved on to licking her empty plate. The kid loved spaghetti sauce.

Daddy rubbed my shoulder. "There are no exercises to help her hearing to improve. There's no operation that can fix her ears.”

“Then how can she learn to talk?” Paul clamped his hands over his ears and watched Mom’s answer in an attempt to drown out sound and read our lips.

“She’ll go to a special school, but for now, we can teach her words at home like Debbie’s been doing already.” Once again, Mom attempted an encouraging smile. She turned her attention to Krista, using a wadded-up napkin to wipe down spaghetti-covered cheeks.

Wade’s face lit up. “Remember next door, when the Gastons’ cousin came to visit from Germany, and he didn’t know English? We’d point to things and say what they were, and he’d repeat it. We can do that for Krista.”

Wade had the right idea. We’d say words and act them out to let her know what we were doing or what we planned to do. She was smart. She’d figure it out. And we’d all learn sign language.

Krista raised her arms for someone to let her out of the highchair. See? She communicated.

I lifted her and tried to settle her on my lap, but she slid to the floor. Little hands and knees became a blur of motion as she crawled away at top speed and then looked back at us with a sparkling grin that said, *Catch me if you can.*

Wade accepted the challenge, and he chased her down the hall on *his* hands and knees. Her shrieks of laughter bounced off the walls.

Mom stacked dirty plates with a gentle clatter. Paul grabbed the last slice of garlic bread. A sweet scent of cherry-vanilla wafted through the room as Daddy lit his pipe. Normal family things.

As I sauntered out of the kitchen in search of my latest Trixie Belden book, Krista crawled to me and hugged my legs. I swung her to my hip. We whirled and dipped, waltzing around the living room. When I stopped to catch my breath, she placed little hands on either side of my face. Sparkling eyes and a wide smile told me she was delighted to be home.

We rubbed noses, *Eskimo kisses,* my grandma called them.

"Okay, little sister, you're well on your way.

"Leg braces, hearing aids, this is your day

"To walk and to talk until someday you'll hear

"The sounds of this world in your own little ear."

Paul smacked my shoulder as he walked past me. "You're a regular Dr. Seuss."

I called after him. "If *you* recognized his style, then I did a good job."

Krista giggled and rubbed her cheek against mine. As if she understood every word we said.

Book Discussion Questions

I wrote the World Without Sound series in order to share my family's experiences as we learned to navigate the strange new world of the Deaf community. Nobody even used that phrase—Deaf community or Deaf Culture—back in the 1960s!

The following questions can be answered by both adults and middle grade/high school students.

WHAT IF?

What if you were in Debbie's place as she and her family tried to figure out how to help Krista to communicate with them? Would you do the same things Debbie did for her sister? Can you think of other things you might do to help the baby that Debbie didn't do?

QUESTIONS

1. In the first chapter, Debbie couldn't believe *anything* would be "wrong" with the new baby. If your parents had warned you that a new baby in the family would have health problems, what would you be thinking? What would you do?
2. . Since Debbie is the daughter of an Air Force pilot,

she has had to move many times—and she's only twelve. If you have had to move often, how did you cope with the changes? If you have *not* had to move often, how do you think you would handle a new home, new friends, and new school every one to three years?

3. What was the hardest thing about moving away from Francie? What might be some good things about moving to a new home?

4. When baby Krista arrives home right after she's born, Debbie compares the big brothers and sister as a *deluge*. Why was *deluge* a good word to use in describing them?

5. Debbie does not want to hand baby Krista to her father as they prepare to drive to the hospital. Why? If you were Debbie, would you have felt the same way?

6. Do you agree with Debbie that children need bright colors surrounding them if they must stay in a hospital? Why or why not?

7. Have you ever had to stay in a hospital? What was it like? What would you tell another kid who had to have an operation—any tips?

8. In the 1960s, the term "mentally retarded" was a medical diagnosis. That is not the case today. How did you feel when Debbie first used the term and explained it?

9. Debbie entered junior high school without a best friend to depend on.

ADULT READERS: Think back to your own middle school/junior high years. What makes change so difficult at that age?

STUDENT READERS: What is the hardest thing about middle school/junior high school and your social life?

10. Decades ago, doctors did not encourage parents to

work at improving the situation of a child with disabilities. Why do you think they did this?

11. Today, kids deal with cyber bullying. Debbie didn't have to endure that, but people are people, no matter if it's 2023 or 1844 or 27 B.C.! Debbie decides to face down a bully when he is mean to someone else. Would you have had the courage to tell a bully to stop hurting people?

12. After she yells at the bully, she feels terrible. Why?

13. Why was saying goodbye to Nancy different from all the other times Debbie had to say goodbye to her friends?

14. How did you feel about Jimmy the second time Debbie bumped into him ? Why did you choose that feeling?

15. Debbie felt like her summer camp experience was ruined when she and Francie couldn't stay in the same cabin. Would you have felt the same way, or would you have tried harder to find new friends?

16. What was your reaction when Debbie told the doctor his services were "no longer required?"

17. What was your opinion of Debbie's attitude on the ski trip?

18. There are several scenes throughout the book that show how all four of the brothers and sisters played together. Which scene was your favorite? Why?

19. As Debbie faces more problems near the end of the book, she compares herself to a soldier preparing for battle. Why do you think she would use that analogy?

20. In the final chapter, Debbie learns that Krista is deaf and has cerebral palsy. Why does Debbie seem happy about this news? (Hint: read the last two pages again.)

ENJOY THE FIRST CHAPTER OF *DANCING INTO SILENCE*, BOOK 2

Chapter 1:
The Best Thing and the Worst Thing
(February 1967)

Last summer, Fwan-nee
Saved me from dogs in a barn.
I like Fwan-nee now.

Leaf shadows danced in the sliver of a moonbeam reflected on the bedroom wall. I yawned and snuggled under the covers while Francie fussed with her pillow on the other side of the room. The best thing in the world was this moment, getting to visit my oldest friend for three whole days.

"Debbie?"

"Mm-hmm."

The heat ticking through the baseboards created a cozy lullaby.

"We haven't talked about the *worst* thing."

Francie and I used to have sleepovers every Friday night when I lived around the block, and we always talked about the best thing and the worst thing of the week.

I'd spent the last month *ignoring* the worst thing in my life.

"Now or later?" Her voice died to a whisper.

"Now. Then we can get up tomorrow and have

fun."

Like killing mold by exposing it to sunlight, we needed to toss out all of our sadness where we could see it clearly instead of letting it lurk in dim corners. Then *maybe* we could enjoy the rest of my stay.

Francie turned on the bedside lamp, creating a soft glow from the milk glass. "I'll start."

Even after she'd crushed her honey-brown hair on the pillow, it draped silky and smooth over one shoulder. My frizzy blond waves never looked that good.

Francie's deep blue eyes glittered with tears. "My dad has a new job, and we're moving to Idaho."

Back in January, she'd told me the news over the phone. It sounded even worse in person. Worse than when I had to move to the opposite end of New York State after fifth grade. Now, we'd live even farther apart. Who could take time for a road trip across the country? And nobody was rich enough to fly. We might not ever see each other again.

I stared at the Beatles poster on the wall above the dresser. John Lennon, who always seemed to brood over the problems in life, peered back at me. My old Tressy doll sat on top of the dresser. Her perky smile created an odd contrast with his solemn expression. "What's the worst thing about moving?"

Francie's tears spilled over. "I'll never see Ernie again."

I'd feel the same way if my boyfriend, Chip, was gone from my life forever. "Are you going to write to each other?"

"Probably. But I haven't told him yet. What if he breaks up with me *now* so it won't hurt so bad later?"

"If he's that much of a weenie, he's not good enough for you."

She hiccupped a laugh through her tears and sniffed. "Thanks."

"What's the best thing about moving?"

Paul McCartney's face smiled at me from the poster. His upbeat personality kicked aside John's glum attitude.

She thought for a moment. "I'll get to ski in the Rocky Mountains. They'll make the Adirondacks feel like bunny hills."

"Then I'd better not visit you in winter."

Francie snorted. She knew I was terrified of skiing. "We'd have to be on the lookout for bears in the summer."

"Better than swimming with sharks, right?" *She* was terrified of the ocean.

Our giggles brought a parental voice from the other side of the wall. "Girls."

Francie turned off the lamp. Your turn," she whispered. "Worst thing."

All of my laughter drained away. "We're moving to California next month so my dad can train for Vietnam." The idea of my father being in danger every day for a whole year hovered over me like a dark parachute descending to the ground and burying me underneath folds of fear.

In the moonlight, her eyes widened. "Will he have to bomb villages?"

"I don't know. I think he's supposed to shoot enemy planes."

We never talked about these things at home. I couldn't picture my father killing anybody. He was the nicest, kindest dad in the world, but…he was a fighter pilot.

"Have you seen all the protests on the news?" Francie was full of uncomfortable questions.

"We try not to watch." What if she was like the people on TV, screaming and swearing at any man in a uniform? Would she hate me because my dad was in the Air Force? "What do *you* think of the war protests?"

She shook her head. "I don't know. Those people are so nasty. But I guess I do wonder why we're in a war at all."

How had Daddy explained it?

"Before we were born, communists in North Korea tried to take over South Korea, and we went to war to stop them. Now, communists in North Vietnam are trying to take over South Vietnam, and we have to do it again."

"Why not just let them be communist?"

"Because the people in the south don't want to be, and we're their friends. If we don't help our friends, they'll lose the war, and then the communists will try to take over Cambodia and Burma and Laos and Thailand."

"And those people don't want to be communist either, I guess." Silence for a few seconds while she paused to consider strangers halfway around the world. "What's the worst thing about moving to California?"

"My dad could die."

If I didn't want to watch the news, and I didn't want to think about what my dad might have to do in a war, I sure didn't want to think about him dying. I'd never even said those words out loud before. To stop Francie from asking any more questions, I rushed on with my list of "next-worsts."

"Then there's other stuff like I won't see Chip for months. I'll have to make new friends and then leave almost as soon as I've gotten to know them. Without Dad around to referee, my mother will drive me crazy. But I'm the oldest kid, so I'll be expected to help out, especially with Krista. What if I mess up?" I paused for breath. "And I'll be living in a desert with rattlesnakes, scorpions, black widows, and who knows what else that can kill a person."

I didn't appreciate Francie's snicker.

"If it were that dangerous, *nobody* would survive in California. There's an awful lot of people there."

"Maybe, but I'll be praying for angels to protect me every night while I sleep."

"You do that." The smile remained in her voice. "What's the best thing?"

Easy answer. "After four months, I get to go back home to Hampton Shores and the ocean."

"That doesn't count. What's the best thing in *California?*"

Linda Sammaritan writes realistic fiction, mostly for kids ages ten to fourteen.

Linda always figured she'd teach teens and tweens for sixty-five years, at which point, school authorities would present her with a retirement wheelchair and roll her out the door. However, God changed those plans when He gave her a growing passion for writing fiction. In May of 2016, she blew goodbye kisses to her students and dedicated her work hours to becoming an author.

A wife, mother of three, and grandmother to eight, Linda regales the youngest grandchildren with "Nona Stories," tales of her childhood. Maybe one day those stories will be in picture books!

Where Linda can be found on the web:
www.lindasammaritan.com
www.facebook.com/lindasammaritan
www.twitter.com/LindaSammaritan
www.instagram.com/lindasammaritan

www.ingramcontent.com/pod-product-compliance
Lightning Source LLC
Chambersburg PA
CBHW070451200726
48293CB00007B/2167